"Pretty cool hiding spot," Cordelia said, crouching so she would be at the boy's eye level when he turned around. "Maybe we should head back. Your mom and dad are probably looking for you."

The boy didn't move. Cordelia inched closer.

"They're probably worried sick," Cordelia said, reaching out to gently touch his shoulder. "Besides, it's a beautiful day! Don't you want to go—"

Her hand passed through the boy's shoulder as though it wasn't there.

A cold, stinging feeling spread throughout her fingers, like she had buried them in snow. The boy rose to his feet and turned around. He wore thick glasses over his blue eyes, which were wide with surprise, as though Cordelia was the incorporeal one. The wheels of Cordelia's mind spun uselessly, like a toy train off its tracks, trying to make sense of what was happening.

He's a . . . a . . .

J. A. WHITE

SHADOW SCHOOL

ARCHIMANCY

KATHERINE TEGEN BOOKS
An Imprint of HarperCollins Publishers

For Yeeshing
Always

Katherine Tegen Books is an imprint of HarperCollins Publishers.

Shadow School #1: Archimancy
Copyright © 2019 by J. A. White

Library of Congress Cataloging-in-Publication Data

Names: White, J. A., author
Title: Archimancy / J. A. White.
Description: First edition. | New York, NY : Katherine Tegen Books, an imprint of
   HarperCollinsPublishers, [2019] | Series: Shadow school ; #1 | Summary: Sixth-
   graders Cordelia, Agnes, and Benji go on a quest to unravel the secrets of Shadow
   School.
Identifiers: LCCN 2018056407 | ISBN 978-0-06-283829-2 (paperback)
Subjects: | CYAC: Middle schools–Fiction. | Schools–Fiction. | Ghosts–Fiction. |
   Haunted places–Fiction. | BISAC: JUVENILE FICTION / Fantasy & Magic. |
   JUVENILE FICTION / Monsters. | JUVENILE FICTION / School & Education.
Classification: LCC PZ7.W58327 Arc 2019 | DDC [Fic]–dc23 LC record available at
   https://lccn.loc.gov/2018056407

Typography by Andrea Vandergrift
21 22 23 24   PC/BRR   10 9 8 7 6 5 4 3 2
❖
First paperback edition, 2020

ALSO BY J. A. WHITE

Nightbooks

The Thickety
A Path Begins
The Whispering Trees
Well of Witches
The Last Spell

CONTENTS

1

The Man at the Window

Cordelia Liu stared up at her new school in disbelief.

It looked more like a creepy old mansion than a place of learning. Everything was eerily symmetrical, as though the school had been unfolded from the pages of a pop-up storybook. There were several conical towers on the left side of the building and their exact twins on the right, along with a matching assortment of gables and turrets. At the precise center of the school, an arched window several stories high split the exterior like a gaping wound.

A copper plate set into the bricks read:

ELIJAH Z. SHADOW MIDDLE SCHOOL
GRADES 5–8
KNOWLEDGE. CHARACTER. SPIRIT.

Until this point, Cordelia hadn't realized that there was a longer version of the school's name; the locals simply called it Shadow School. She was surprised—and a little relieved—that it had been named after a real person. Last night, her dreams had been haunted by teachers with shadowy faces.

This Elijah Shadow is probably the rich guy who donated the building, she thought, feeling silly. *Boring dude, spooky name. Nothing more than that.*

Cordelia shivered. The windbreaker she was wearing had been warm enough back in California, but it was hopelessly out of its league here in New Hampshire. She started to join the crowd of students entering the school but noticed a man in a gray suit watching her from one of the upper windows. It was hard to read his expression from this distance, but his shoulders were slumped. *Guess I'm not the only one who doesn't want to be here*, Cordelia thought, figuring the man was a teacher with some old-fashioned ideas about how to dress. She gave a little wave, not wanting to appear rude.

The man's mouth fell open, as though he couldn't believe that she had actually acknowledged him. Instead of simply waving in return, however, he slammed his hands flat against the window and stared down at her with disquieting intensity.

Cordelia shivered. This time, it had nothing to do with the weather.

What's wrong with that guy? she wondered, turning away from his blank-faced stare. She hurried toward the front of the school, seeking warmth and voices. Just before she passed through the entrance, Cordelia risked a second glance at the window. The man was gone.

2

Mr. Derleth and Mrs. Aickman

For a moment, Cordelia wondered if she had somehow walked into the wrong building. The walls of the high-ceilinged foyer were papered with a gold-and-white pattern, which perfectly complemented the cranberry red of the carpet. Bronze sconces illuminated the halls. A wide staircase with chestnut railings wound its way to the second floor.

This can't really be a school, Cordelia thought.

Upon further inspection, however, she noticed more familiar details: a sign for the main office, teachers sharing a quick chat before class began, brightly decorated bulletin boards. The building looked like the home of a creepy old spinster, but at its heart beat a normal, everyday school.

Cordelia had received her schedule in the mail and knew her homeroom teacher was Mr. Derleth in room 211. After nearly colliding with a woman glued to her phone, she climbed the stairs to a wide hallway with royal blue walls. Cordelia checked the room number in front of her—234—and the room to its immediate right—233—and followed the descending numbers beneath a series of evenly spaced arches. It was quieter than her old school. Not only did the carpet muffle footsteps, but the students themselves spoke with hushed voices, as though they suspected someone might be eavesdropping at all times. Cordelia imagined what the first day at Ridgewood would be like right now, her best friends Mabel and Ava walking arm in arm through a glorious cacophony of rowdy students—before remembering, with a jolt, that California was three hours behind New Hampshire. Mabel and Ava were still asleep.

Cordelia suddenly felt more alone than ever, separated from her former life not only by distance but time.

When she got to room 215, Cordelia figured that she was almost there, but the numbers suddenly dropped all pretense of consistency: 215 was followed by 242 and then, for some unfathomable reason, 32A. Cordelia's homeroom—211—was nowhere to be found. She considered retracing her steps and then decided that she'd better ask for help instead.

"Excuse me," Cordelia asked a passing girl who was walking alone, pulling a rolling backpack like a traveler at the airport. "Do you know where room 211 is?"

The girl checked over her shoulder, as if Cordelia couldn't possibly be talking to her. She was sturdy looking, with deep-set green eyes and blond hair tied in a pragmatic ponytail. Her flannel shirt was untucked.

"I'm going to room 211," the girl said. "We must be in the same homeroom. Mr. Derleth?"

Cordelia nodded.

"We can walk together, if you'd like," the girl suggested.

"Cool. I'm Cordelia."

"Agnes."

They started down the hallway. Agnes was a lot taller than Cordelia—no great achievement there—but walked with a timid, guarded gait.

"I don't remember seeing you last year," Agnes said. "You must be new."

"First day."

"Getting around Shadow School can be tricky if you don't know where you're going. That's not a problem for me. I have a particularly strong entorhinal region. That's the part of the brain that controls your sense of direction. How's your entorhinal region?"

"I never really thought about it."

"That must be nice," Agnes said. "I think about everything. Even when I don't want to. My mom says my brain is like a neighbor who plays their music too loud and won't turn it down no matter how nicely you ask. I'm sorry. We just met. I should be asking about you." She stared intently into the air, as though cycling through a list of possible questions. "Do you have any nut allergies?" she finally asked.

Cordelia shook her head. "I love nuts."

Agnes smiled, revealing light blue braces.

"Me too! Even peanuts. Which aren't actually nuts. They're legumes. But pealegume doesn't really roll off the tongue, does it?"

"Not really," Cordelia said, unsure what to make of this strange girl. "Is Mr. Derleth nice?"

"I don't know," said Agnes. "He's new. Shadow School always has a lot of new teachers at the beginning of the year. The old ones tend to find different jobs over the summer. Or sometimes they don't even make it through the year. Our second math teacher last year walked out in the middle of a lesson and we never saw her again. I think they find the school creepy."

They passed an oil painting of a little girl wearing an old-fashioned nightdress. A teddy bear leaking black stuffing dangled from her hand.

"Can't imagine why," Cordelia muttered.

They entered an open area. There was no carpet here. Instead, tessellating triangles tiled the floor. A young teacher wearing a pretty dress that seemed too fancy for school checked her appearance in an antique floor mirror.

"This place is huge!" Cordelia exclaimed.

"You'll get used to it," Agnes said. "But you shouldn't wander off by yourself until you get your bearings. And don't go to the third or fourth floor. It's like a maze. Sixth graders don't have any classes up there, anyway."

"Good to know," Cordelia said.

"I can be your guide today and make sure you get to class on time." Agnes paused awkwardly and tugged on the bottom of her shirt. "But only if you want to. I understand if you'd rather find someone else. I would probably want to find someone else if I was—"

"I'd love for you to be my guide," Cordelia said, and was surprised to find that she meant it. Agnes was a little odd, but she was starting to like her.

They found room 211 between room 239 and a supply closet. Except for the desks and blackboard, it looked more like a living room than a classroom, with wood-paneled walls, a fireplace, and a long black couch in the back of the room. Cordelia slid into the first unoccupied seat she saw, aware that some of the students were watching her with mild interest; she was, after all, the new girl. Agnes, head down, continued to the back of the room. No one acknowledged her at all.

"Good morning," Mr. Derleth said with a slight Southern twang. He was a tall man with a neatly trimmed beard and the saddest eyes that Cordelia had ever seen. His clothes hung off his gangly body. "My name is Mr. Derleth. I'll be your homeroom teacher and your social studies teacher as well. I look forward to our year together."

As Mr. Derleth took attendance, Cordelia tried to match names to faces. Nolan Bluth was a shaggy-haired boy losing the war against acne. Francesca Calvino didn't hear her name the first time because her nose was buried in a book. Mason James, a smug-looking boy with brown hair dyed red at its tips, responded "Not here!" instead of "Here!" and immediately high-fived his friends, who were all wearing the same football jerseys as he was. Mr. Derleth glanced up and then decided to ignore them, as though their behavior was too tiresome to correct.

After the pledge, a final student strode into the room with his hands jammed deep into his pockets. He was wearing a black hoodie and walked with his head down. Cordelia caught a glimpse of long hair and dark eyes.

"Benji Núñez, I assume?" Mr. Derleth asked,

checking his attendance list.

The boy gave a quick nod and took a seat behind Cordelia. Mr. Derleth leaned against his desk, which was completely bereft of the usual teacher knickknacks and family photos, and stared out at their expectant faces. There was a distant look in his eyes, as though he wasn't really seeing them at all.

"This is an impressive building," he said. "It looks like something you'd need a ticket to enter, like one of those old mansions in Rhode Island. I have no idea how the town managed to afford such a fancy public school, but—"

A girl raised her hand. Cordelia tried to remember her name. *Maria? Melissa?*

"Yes, Miranda," Mr. Derleth said.

"My father is on the board of education," she said. "And he told me that the town doesn't pay a cent for this school. The Shadow family owns the building, but they ran out of money and couldn't afford the taxes anymore, so instead of losing their property altogether, they made a deal. They wouldn't have to pay taxes, and in exchange the town could use the building as a public school. My dad says that as part of the agreement, the school isn't allowed to change anything about the original structure because it's all historical and stuff. That's why everything looks so old-fashioned."

Mr. Derleth listened to this information with his head down and eyes half closed. Cordelia thought it was because he was tired—judging from the swollen sacks beneath his eyes, Mr. Derleth and sleep were nodding acquaintances at best—but it turned out that this was just his way of focusing.

"That's interesting, Miranda," he said. "And I'm so happy that Shadow School is being preserved. I spent a few evenings at the Ludlow Historical Society this summer to assuage my idle curiosity. Shadow School's history is extraordinary, to say the least. Perhaps, as the year goes on, you can teach me some local stories that can't be found in any book. I'd love to learn as much about this fascinating place as possible."

The morning bell rang, ending homeroom. As the students rose from their seats, Mr. Derleth held up a hand, holding them at bay.

"Just a few quick announcements before you head off to language arts," he said, consulting a sticky note. "If you owe the office any forms, please see that they get them by Friday. Band won't begin for two more weeks, but you should email Ms. Schwerin about instrument rentals if you haven't already done so. Dr. Roqueni would like to remind you that our custodial staff locks up at five o'clock sharp. Students are not permitted inside the school after dark. No exceptions. Today's lunch special is macaroni and cheese." Mr. Derleth offered the vaguest hint of a smile. "Enjoy your day."

Mrs. Aickman's language arts classroom was dark and dreary. Paper tombstones covered a bulletin board at the back of the room. The "deceased" were all famous poets. Cordelia saw Poe, Dickinson, and Shakespeare, among others. Stenciled letters proclaimed: *THEIR WORDS LIVE. THEY DO NOT.*

Mrs. Aickman herself was a diminutive woman with blue eyes and spiky gray hair. She waved the students inside the room, bracelets jangling together on her thin wrists.

"Morning," she said, pacing back and forth. "You'll notice I did not say 'Good morning.' I would never be so presumptuous. One of you brave children might be in the midst of some terrible tragedy. Perhaps your family received a phone call in the middle of the night, informing you of a favorite relative's untimely demise. Or maybe Mr. Whiskers—that sweet, gentle cat—got splatted by a truck! No morning is ever 'good,' not for everyone." She held her hand to her heart. "And that pain . . . is a *miracle.* Because great literature can only come from heartache and misery! Now, which one of you is Cordelia?"

Cordelia reluctantly raised her hand. Chairs squeaked

as the other students turned to face her. She fought the urge to hide beneath her desk.

"I'm dying to know," Mrs. Aickman said. "Are you named after the Cordelia in *King Lear*?" She addressed the class as a whole. "That's a famous play by William Shakespeare. A *tragedy*."

Cordelia nodded politely. It wasn't the first time she had been asked this question.

"My parents met in a Shakespeare class back in college," she said.

"How dreadfully romantic," replied Mrs. Aickman. "In the play, class, Cordelia is the king's kind, dutiful daughter. She has two *terrible* sisters, however. Goneril and Regan." She raised her eyebrows at Cordelia. "Any evil sisters at home?"

"Just me."

"Pity. You would have had so many interesting things to write about during our personal narrative unit. Speaking of which, it's always good to begin a new year with a bit of writing, so please take out your notebooks and"—Benji Núñez slipped into the room, head down, and took a seat. Mrs. Aickman gave him a quick look of disapproval and continued—"write a page or two about your saddest summer memory."

Agnes raised her hand.

"I'm sorry," she said. "Just to clarify—did you say

'saddest' summer memory?"

"That's correct."

"But my summer was *wonderful*," Miranda chimed in. "My family has this gorgeous lake house in Maine, and every day we—"

Mrs. Aickman made a loud snoring noise.

"No one wants to read about happy people," the teacher said. "In order to truly move a reader, you need to tap a spile deep into your soul and let the pain drip free. Bad vacations! Hideous sunburns! Dead relatives! That's the good stuff!"

The students took out their notebooks and got to work. Cordelia considered herself a mediocre writer at best, but for this particular assignment, the words flowed easily. She started with the moment her parents told her they were moving—using tons of exclamation points to convey her shock and dismay—and then wrote about all the friends she had left behind in California. In her final sentences, Cordelia described how she had woken up that first chilly morning in New Hampshire and cried into her pillow, knowing that her old life was over forever.

When she was done, Cordelia closed her notebook and waited for her classmates to finish. She heard two boys whispering to her right.

"I touched the attic door yesterday," said the first

boy. He was the one with the red tips in his hair. Mason, Cordelia remembered.

"No way," said the second boy, who had freckles and a long, horsey face. Cordelia didn't remember his name. "School wasn't even open."

"Not to students," Mason said. "But all the teachers had to be here setting up their rooms. It's the law. No one noticed me sneaking up to the fourth floor."

The second boy nodded with respect.

"Was it hot, like they say?"

"Burning." Mason dropped his voice to an even softer whisper. "And that's not all. When I put my ear close to the door I heard this crackling noise, like a campfire."

"You're making that up," the boy said. Cordelia could hear the fear in his voice.

"Go up there yourself if you don't believe me," Mason said.

"Maybe I will."

"You won't. You're too scared, just like everyone else. Another thing—the moment my hand touched the doorknob, I heard this horrible scream. It was Elijah Shadow. I'm sure of it. Still burning after all these—"

Mrs. Aickman shushed them, and the boys went back to pretending to write. *What was that all about?* Cordelia thought. She didn't actually *believe* Mason—he was clearly just trying to freak out his gullible friend—but she was curious where the story had come from in the first place.

What happened in the attic?

A few minutes later, Mrs. Aickman announced that she would now be taking volunteers for anyone who wanted to share their essay. Cordelia slouched in her seat, praying the teacher didn't call on her; she had no desire to share her innermost thoughts with a roomful of strangers. Fortunately, plenty of other kids were eager to read their work. Mrs. Aickman selected a boy named Grant Thompson, who strode to the front of the room and then paused a moment to clear his throat before reading.

His essay was entitled "The Summer All My Pets Died."

"My gerbil was the first to go," Grant said in an overdramatic voice. "She wouldn't be the last."

Grant had a lot of pets, and by the fourth backyard funeral, Cordelia's attention had begun to wander. For this reason, she happened to be looking in the right direction when the woman in hospital scrubs passed the open doorway. She wore a surgical mask over her mouth and held her gloved hands in the air, as though she had just scrubbed up for surgery. Cordelia jerked in her chair, startling Agnes.

"Did you see her?" Cordelia whispered, nodding toward the door.

"Who?" Agnes asked.

Cordelia started to explain and then shook her head; Mrs. Aickman was looking their way, and she didn't want to get in trouble on the first day of school. Besides, she had already thought of a perfectly reasonable explanation for the woman's unusual appearance: she was probably a science teacher intent on making a grand entrance on the first day of school. *Everyone here is so weird*, Cordelia thought, slumping in her seat. She pictured the brightly lit corridors of Ridgewood, where the teachers wore normal clothes and the students wrote about happy memories instead of sad ones.

Cordelia missed her old life more than ever.

The Boy Beneath the Bleachers

The day droned on. The rest of Cordelia's teachers were a mixed bag. She liked her art teacher, Ms. Perez, who looked like she was still in high school and gave them chocolate and stickers at the end of class. Their science teacher, Ms. Patel, was also young, but in every other way the polar opposite of Ms. Perez: hyperorganized instead of carefree, strict instead of lenient. Cordelia's least favorite teacher, however, was Mrs. Machen, an ancient crone who genuinely disliked children and looked like she should have retired a decade ago. Mrs. Machen felt that constant practice through worksheets was the only way to improve their math skills, and along those lines assigned a thick packet for homework.

By seventh period, Cordelia needed a break. After the unstructured freedom of summer vacation, it was nearly impossible to sit in a chair all day without getting antsy. Ten minutes into social studies, Cordelia asked to use the bathroom and escaped into the hallway. She walked past the main office and headed down an unexplored corridor with no particular destination in mind, catching snatches of different voices as teachers calmly explained their rules and expectations (except for Mrs. Machen, who was in the process of scolding a terrified fifth grader for forgetting the difference between a numerator and denominator). After she'd taken a few random turns, the school grew quiet. *Guess they have more space than they need*, she thought, peeking through the window of the nearest door. A single chair sat in the center of the dark room.

Cordelia backed away.

A few turns later she found herself in a short, doorless hallway—a dead end. There was a large photograph on the far wall. Cordelia took a closer look. The photograph showed a gray-haired black man sitting at a drawing table with the sleeves of his shirt rolled up. He seemed unaware that someone was taking his picture, his attention fully focused on his work. There was an obsessive, burning gleam to his eyes that Cordelia found a little frightening.

"The only known photograph of Elijah Shadow," said a voice behind her.

Cordelia gasped in surprise and spun around. The speaker was a tall, elegant woman with light brown skin, her hair piled high in voluminous ringlets.

"I apologize for startling you," she said, holding out her hand. "I'm Dr. Roqueni, the principal here at Shadow School."

Cordelia shook her hand. Dr. Roqueni had a pianist's fingers, long and graceful.

"Cordelia Liu. It's a pleasure to meet you."

"Likewise," Dr. Roqueni said. "Let me take this opportunity to welcome you to our school. I'm sorry I haven't had a chance to meet you until now. There was an orientation for new students this summer, but I guess you couldn't make it."

"We weren't expecting to move," Cordelia said. "But then my dad lost his job, so . . ."

"You had to uproot your entire existence," Dr. Roqueni said with genuine sympathy. "That's rough, Cordelia. Trust me; I know. Where are you from?"

"Just outside San Francisco."

"I've always dreamed of seeing the West Coast," Dr. Roqueni said with a wistful expression. "Is it as nice as people say?"

"Nicer."

"Well, California's loss is our gain. We might not have beaches, but Ludlow isn't such a bad little town. And I'm sure you'll be happy here at Shadow School. What do you think so far?"

"Umm," Cordelia said, not wanting to offend the principal. "It's not quite what I expected."

"You mean your old school wasn't a creepy old Victorian mansion?" Dr. Roqueni asked in mock surprise.

Cordelia smiled and shook her head.

"This building was never meant to be a school," Dr. Roqueni said. She pointed to the photograph of Elijah Shadow. "It was actually his house. Elijah designed it himself. Anyone tell you about the attic yet?"

"I overheard two boys in my class talking about it."

"Let me guess," Dr. Roqueni said. "Burning-hot door? Crackle of flames? Screams of agony?"

"Pretty much."

"Our school's own personal urban legend," Dr. Roqueni said. "Elijah Shadow's ghost haunts the attic where he died, and if you dare to open the door, he'll wrap his arms around you and drag you into flames that burn forever." Dr. Roqueni laughed. "It's ridiculous, of course, but I actually don't mind. Kids shouldn't be going up there anyway. The attic's dangerous. It was never properly repaired after the fire."

"So there really was a fire?" Cordelia asked.

"Oh yes," Dr. Roqueni said. "And that *is* how Elijah Shadow died. There's usually some grain of truth to these things. But the rest—" Dr. Roqueni's phone vibrated in her hand. She checked the screen and frowned. "Sorry. There's something that requires my attention. Will you be able to find your way back to class?"

"Totally," said Cordelia, who felt the urge to impress the principal.

"It was lovely talking to you," Dr. Roqueni said. She walked a few steps away and then turned back to face her. "Who's your homeroom teacher?"

"Mr. Derleth."

"One of the new hires," Dr. Roqueni said. Her face grew serious. "Did he remember to tell you that all students need to be out of the school by nightfall?"

Cordelia nodded.

"Excellent," Dr. Roqueni said. "Just wanted to double-check."

As Cordelia attempted to retrace her path back to social studies, she thought about what she had learned. *A man died in this school. And people think his ghost haunts the attic.* She wanted to believe that it was just a silly story, like Dr. Roqueni said. On the other hand, Shadow School sure looked like a haunted mansion, and it was very strange that no one was allowed in the building after dark. *Maybe that's when Elijah Shadow comes down from the attic, roaming the halls and looking for someone to join him forever . . .*

Cordelia was so distracted by these thoughts that she didn't pay close enough attention to where she was going. In a few minutes, she found herself in a part of the school she didn't recognize at all. *My entorhinal region is the worst*, Cordelia thought. There wasn't even anyone that she could ask for directions. The hallways were completely empty, the classrooms dark.

She heard someone crying.

It was definitely a student, though Cordelia couldn't tell if it was a boy or a girl. She didn't think they were hurt. These weren't the quick, breathless tears of someone in physical pain, but a low, rhythmic weeping. It was the kind of crying you allowed yourself when no one else was listening. Wanting to help, she followed the sound to a windowless gym that had seen better days. The floor was buckled in several sections. Only a few flickering ceiling lights worked. On the opposite side of the gym was a set of retractable bleachers that could be folded against the wall to create more space, though right now they were pulled out.

The crying was coming from beneath them.

"Hello?" Cordelia asked, crossing the floor of the gym. "Is everything okay?"

She stepped around the side of the bleachers and peeked through the open end. A small boy of about four or five was kneeling in the shadows, his shoulders heaving as he wept. He wore navy blue pajamas. The pants were patterned with different trains, while the T-shirt featured a green-and-blue locomotive.

Poor little guy, Cordelia thought, her heart melting. She ducked her head and stepped beneath the bleachers.

"Hey there," she said, speaking softly so she didn't scare him. "My name's Cordelia. I'm eleven. How old are you?"

The boy didn't turn around, but she thought his weeping might have grown just a tiny bit softer. Taking this as an invitation, Cordelia halved the distance between them. It was a slow process. The space beneath the bleachers was tight and cramped.

An unexpected thought froze her in place.

What is he doing here?

Shadow School started at fifth grade. The boy couldn't possibly be a student. So who was he? And why was he wearing pajamas and not regular clothes?

Pinpricks of fear ran up and down her arm.

Stop being such a wuss, she scolded herself. *He's just a little boy who got lost somehow. He needs your help.*

"Pretty cool hiding spot," Cordelia said, crouching so she would be at the boy's eye level when he turned around. "Maybe we should head back. Your mom and dad are probably looking for you."

The boy didn't move. Cordelia inched closer.

"They're probably worried sick," Cordelia said, reaching out to gently touch his shoulder. "Besides, it's a beautiful day! Don't you want to go—"

Her hand passed through the boy's shoulder as though it wasn't there.

A cold, stinging feeling spread throughout her fingers, like she had buried them in snow. The boy rose to his feet and turned around. He wore thick glasses over his blue eyes, which were wide with surprise, as though Cordelia was the incorporeal one. The wheels of Cordelia's mind spun uselessly, like a toy train off its tracks, trying to make sense of what was happening.

He's a . . . a . . .

The boy took a step toward her. Cordelia tried to move, but her legs had been injected with rubber, and she fell to the floor. The boy leaned forward and gazed at her with a curious expression, then reached out a hand to touch her face. Cordelia watched it approach, frozen in fear.

She screamed.

The boy covered his ears and turned his back to her. Without waiting to see what he might do next, Cordelia crab-walked along the wooden floor and into the flickering lights, stopping only when she was on the other side of the gym. She watched the bleachers carefully, waiting for the boy to come out and continue the chase. He didn't.

Cordelia slowly got to her feet, trying to wrap her mind around what had happened.

I just saw a ghost, she thought.

As she stumbled out of the gym, Cordelia heard sobbing. She looked back at the bleachers, thinking that it was the boy again. Then she realized that the sobs belonged to her.

4

Listen

The moment her parents got home from work, Cordelia dragged them into the living room and told them the entire story. She expected sympathy. Hugs. Promises that they would return to California on the first available flight.

Instead, her mother let out a long, disappointed sigh and said, "Cordelia, you've made it perfectly clear that you don't want to go to Shadow School, but—a *ghost*? Really?"

"I'm telling the truth," Cordelia insisted, her voice trembling.

To those who didn't know them well, Cordelia's parents seemed like an odd match. Her mom was tall, thin, and Caucasian. Her father was short, pudgy, and Chinese. Mrs. Liu was a social butterfly who had already made a dozen friends in their new town. Mr. Liu barely spoke at all. Despite their differences, they laughed often and rarely argued, especially when it came to their only child.

Her parents looked at each other now, an unspoken understanding passing between them.

"It's not that we don't believe you, sweetie," Mrs. Liu said, brushing back a strand of blond hair. "Or, at least, it's not that we don't believe that *you* believe you saw something. It's just . . ."

"Ghosts aren't real," Mr. Liu said.

Cordelia inhaled deeply in an attempt to control her growing frustration. In terms of appearance, she looked more like her father. Her temper, however, came straight from her mom.

"I know what I saw," Cordelia said.

"And we know how much you wanted to stay in California," Mrs. Liu replied. "You tell me—what makes more sense? That you saw a creepy shadow and *imagined* a ghost—which gives you a reason to skip out on your new school? Or that you saw an actual ghost?"

"I didn't *imagine* anything," Cordelia insisted, her cheeks growing flushed. "I saw a real—"

"This move has been hard for you," Mrs. Liu said.

28

She saw her husband looking down at the floor and touched his arm. "For *all* of us. But this is our home now. The sooner you accept that, the sooner you can start enjoying your new life."

"Fine!" Cordelia exclaimed, rising to her feet. "Don't believe me! But I'm not going back to that school! And you can't make me!"

"Sure we can," Mrs. Liu said cheerfully. "We're your parents. Making you do things is basically our job description."

Cordelia stomped into her new bedroom. It was half the size of her old room and smelled like mothballs. She hated it. Boxes were piled everywhere. They had moved six weeks ago, but Cordelia steadfastly refused to unpack.

It's not fair, she thought, throwing herself onto the bed. *Why don't they believe me?*

After she got bored of feeling sorry for herself, Cordelia checked Instagram, longing for news from the real world. It was a mistake. Seeing how happy her friends looked only made her more depressed. The worst photo was a shot of Ava and Mabel in their first-day outfits, smiling fiercely at the camera. Cordelia felt a sharp pang of jealousy in the pit of her stomach.

They don't miss me at all, she thought, tossing her phone away.

To get her mind off things, Cordelia pulled out her battered old Chromebook and started reading everything she could about ghosts. A lot of the websites were clearly nonsense, but the more reputable ones agreed that ghosts usually haunted a specific location for one of two reasons—either the spirit had lived there when they were alive, or they died there.

The boy definitely didn't live in Shadow School, Cordelia thought. *He's too young to even be a student.*

Which means he died there.

Cordelia took a moment to steel herself for the next step of her investigation, afraid of what she might find. Finally, she googled "Shadow School death." Most of the links led to information about Elijah Shadow, who had indeed died in a fire back in 1929—there were even a few black-and-white photographs of the damaged building to prove it. Cordelia learned little else about the architect himself; he had led, as one writer described it, a "remarkably private life." The links that didn't involve Elijah Shadow dealt with a custodian named David Fisher. He had worked at Shadow School for over a year before disappearing in 2007. Perhaps he hadn't died, but he had certainly never been heard from again.

There was nothing about the boy beneath the bleachers.

Someone knocked on the door, startling her.

"Cordy?" Mrs. Liu asked, peeking her head inside the room. "We're heading into town. Want to come?"

From the moment the moving van had pulled up to their new house, Cordelia's parents had worked hard to sell her on the wonders of New Hampshire. They took a scenic drive through the White Mountains, went kayaking on Lake Winnipesaukee, and spent one afternoon trying to track down as many covered bridges as possible. Cordelia hated every minute of it. The worst part was "downtown" Ludlow, a single strip of lame shops and restaurants with an honest-to-god general store.

"You guys go," Cordelia said. "I have homework."

"On the first day of school?"

Cordelia shrugged.

"We're getting ice cream," Mrs. Liu tried. "It's homemade."

"Mitchell's is better," Cordelia replied. They had stopped there for ice cream whenever they went into San Francisco. "Besides, I'm going to Skype Ava and Mabel in a few minutes. See how things are back home."

"This is your home, Cordelia."

"I want to tell them what happened today. At least *they'll* believe me."

Mrs. Liu sighed with frustration, as though Cordelia

was somehow the one being unreasonable, and shut the door.

After her parents had left the house, Cordelia tried to contact Ava and Mabel. No one picked up. She slammed the Chromebook shut. *I'll try again in a few minutes*, she thought. *I'm sure they want to talk to me. It's just the time difference that's confusing them. That's all.*

In the meantime, Cordelia stared at the ceiling and considered what she had learned. If anything, it raised more questions than it answered.

The boy wasn't a student at Shadow School. And he didn't die there.

So why the heck is he haunting the place?

Cordelia woke up the next morning in a foul mood. She had been half-asleep by the time her California friends finally returned her Skype request, and although she understood that there was a three-hour time difference at play, it still left her feeling unwanted. The actual conversation only made things worse. Cordelia tried to tell them about the ghost, but Ava and Mabel kept rambling on about *their* day, *their* teachers, *their* friends, and she couldn't get a word in edgewise. By the time the opportunity finally presented itself, Cordelia no longer felt like sharing.

They've already forgotten about me, she thought, staring

out the window at the small houses set far back from the rural country road. The bus ride took forever, with huge gaps between stops. Since she had no one to talk to, Cordelia took out her drawing pad and colored pencils. Drawing always made her feel better. She did a few quick sketches of things she missed back home. The tiny box garden in their backyard. The sun setting over the ocean. She turned to the next page, allowing her mind to wander, thinking she might draw the carousel at Golden Gate Park.

Instead, she found herself sketching the boy. Train pajamas. Teary eyes.

"Who are you?" Cordelia asked.

Just looking at the drawing brought a rush of terror to her chest. But . . . if the boy had truly meant her harm, why had he been crying? Cordelia felt like she was missing something important. Instead of throwing the sketch out when she got to school, she taped it to the inside of her locker door. She wasn't sure why.

"Hey," Agnes said, squeezing between two chatting girls and joining Cordelia by the locker. Agnes was wearing a bulky green sweater and brown sweatpants. In her hands she held a brownie that had been carefully folded in wax paper and tied with a red ribbon. "My mom said if you want to be someone's friend, bake them something. It shows you mean business. And so

I made this brownie. Actually, I made a whole tray of brownies. You can't just make a brownie on its own. But this was the one I brought to school. I put nuts in it since you said you didn't have any allergies."

"Wow," Cordelia said, stunned. "That was really nice. Thanks."

"You don't have to eat it if you don't—"

"Of course I want to!" Cordelia said, snatching the brownie with a smile. She had skipped breakfast that morning in an effort to make her parents feel bad. "You want half?"

Agnes shook her head.

"I made it for you, not me." She glanced over Cordelia's shoulder at the drawing of the boy. "Whoa! You're wicked talented! Who is that?"

Cordelia considered telling Agnes the truth but quickly rejected the idea. Her own parents thought it was all in her head. Why would a girl she barely knew believe her?

"No one," she said, closing the locker door.

Cordelia absentmindedly munched on the brownie as they walked to homeroom, but not even chocolate could improve her sour mood. They passed through yet another area of the school that was completely new to her. Copper tiles with floral accents decorated the high ceiling, while red velvet curtains, drawn closed,

34

permitted only a hint of sunlight.

"I still can't believe this is a school," Cordelia said, shaking her head.

"You don't know the half of it," Agnes said. "There are all sorts of secret passageways. The supply closet in Ms. Soney's language arts room has a door in the back that leads to a hidden hallway—you actually have to go through the closet to get to some of the seventh-grade classrooms! And Mr. Blender's room has a trapdoor with a ladder that leads down to the library!"

That actually sounded pretty cool to Cordelia, but she was in a bad mood and determined to stay that way.

"I thought Elijah Shadow was some sort of brilliant architect," she said. "Sounds to me like he had no idea what he was doing. My old school made a lot more sense. I never got lost there—not even once." Cordelia paused, recognizing the whiny tone in her voice and hating it. "I overheard some boys talking about the attic yesterday," she said, changing the subject.

"Mason and Reggie. I heard them too. I wouldn't believe a word of it."

"That's what Dr. Roqueni said."

"You told the principal?" Agnes asked in surprise.

"We met in the hallway. It came up. Dr. Roqueni said that attic stuff is just an urban legend."

"I'm sure she's right. Some of the eighth graders

swear they've heard fire crackling on the other side of the attic door, but they're probably just trying to scare the younger kids. I've never gotten close enough to listen for myself. There're all these Do Not Enter signs. I'm not worried about ghosts. I'm worried about getting in trouble."

Agnes sounded nervous just talking about it. *Ava and Mabel would have laughed at those signs and raced to listen first*, Cordelia thought. She looked at Agnes lugging her huge rolling backpack behind her and wondered if the girl had ever broken a rule in her entire life.

"Is everything okay?" Agnes asked. "You seem kind of down today."

"I'm fine," Cordelia said. "I guess I just miss my old friends. They were the coolest, you know." Cordelia grimaced, realizing how bad that sounded, and nudged Agnes with her shoulder. "Not that I don't like my new friend too!"

"It's okay," Agnes said with a look of resignation. "I'm sure your California friends are much cooler than me. I'm not offended."

"I really didn't mean it like that," Cordelia said, turning toward Agnes. "You've been so nice to—"

Since she wasn't looking where she was going, Cordelia didn't see the man coming from the adjoining hallway, and it was up to Agnes to grab her arm before she walked right into him. He was carrying a long wooden plank over one shoulder and holding an orange bucket.

"Watch where you're going, kid!" he snapped.

The custodian was a giant of a man with a bushy gray goatee. Cordelia knew she shouldn't judge people based on appearances, but she couldn't help feeling a little afraid, especially when the custodian leveled his gaze on her. She noticed a scar above his left eyebrow and a second, longer one along the side of his neck.

"Sorry," Cordelia mumbled.

The custodian grunted and continued along his way.

"That's Mr. Ward," Agnes said when he was out of earshot. "I think he's a little scary."

"Me too," Cordelia said, still shaken from the encounter.

"There's a rumor about him," Agnes whispered as they started to walk again. "Years ago, there was another custodian who worked here. One day he just vanished."

"David Fisher," Cordelia said. When Agnes looked at her with surprise, she added, "I got bored last night and did some surfing. They never found out what happened to him, right?"

"Right," Agnes said. "But the night before he vanished, people heard him and Mr. Ward having this big argument."

"What about?"

"No one knows," Agnes said. "But it must have been pretty bad, because the rumor is that Mr. Ward killed David Fisher and burned up the body in the furnace downstairs."

"Seriously?" Cordelia asked in horror.

"It's just a rumor," Agnes said. "There's no actual *evidence*. As far as I'm concerned, Mr. Ward is just a grumpy old man who hates kids. That other stuff is an urban legend, like the attic."

"You're right," Cordelia said. "It's kind of ridiculous if you stop and think about it." On the other hand, she would have laughed at the idea of a ghost just a few days ago, so a murderous school custodian didn't seem *that* far-fetched. At this point, Cordelia didn't know what to believe.

Now that names had been memorized and notebooks labeled, the actual learning began. Ms. Patel broke them into groups for a project on lab safety; Cordelia met a couple of kids she liked, though it was too early to tell if the friendships would stick. Mrs. Aickman discussed an upcoming field trip to the local cemetery, where they would be doing gravestone rubbings and discussing the "poetry of epitaphs." Mrs. Machen gave them a packet. Mr. Derleth did an interesting lesson on how the past shaped the future, though he often got distracted and lost his place, staring out into the distance with his sad brown eyes. Cordelia was having a hard time concentrating as well. Yesterday's fear lingered like a low-grade fever, and she kept glancing up at the open door, certain the boy would be standing there.

She had gym sixth period.

Although her initial instinct was to feign some illness in order to skip the class altogether, Cordelia forced herself to go. *I'll have to eventually*, she thought. *Besides, things will be different with other people there. Ghosts only show up when you're alone.* Nevertheless, it was hard for Cordelia to enter the gym, especially when she saw that the students were sitting on the bleachers.

"Everything okay?" Agnes asked. "You look like you're going to be sick."

"Not a big gym fan," Cordelia said.

She crossed the floor with jittery steps and sat on the edge of the first row, away from any little hands that might try to reach through the cracks and grab her.

"Welcome to physical education," said Mr. Bruce. He looked like he had been an athlete back in his prime, though much of the muscle had run to fat. He was wearing a red jersey with an *A* on it. "Before you ask, I did not attend the University of Alabama, as you might guess from what I'm wearing. I'm not even a fan of the Crimson Tide." He crossed his beefy arms and grinned with obvious pride. "I do, however, own exactly one hundred eighty different sports jerseys. I'll wear a different one every day of the school year, in alphabetical order according to the team's state of origin. When I wear my Minnesota Timberwolves jersey, you'll know we're about halfway through the year. And when you see the Washington Nationals, you can start getting really excited, because summer is right around the corner."

As Mr. Bruce talked, Cordelia tried, as nonchalantly as possible, to peek between the cracks of the bleachers. The boy wasn't there. She felt some of the tension leave her body.

Maybe he hides when there are too many people around, she thought. *Or maybe he's in a different part of the school right now.*

Benji Núñez strolled into the gym, face hidden beneath his hoodie. He hurried past the teacher and found a spot on the bleachers as far from everyone else as possible.

"Benji Núñez," Mr. Bruce said, reaching for his clipboard so he could check off the name. "How nice of you to join us this afternoon. And a mere four minutes late. Not bad!" He mimed the removal of a hood. "You know the rules. Earbuds too."

Benji threw back his hood, revealing long, wavy black hair and a surly expression. He yanked out the earbuds. Cordelia heard a thrumming bass line before he swiped off the music.

How does that boy manage to be late for every single class? Cordelia wondered.

She turned her attention back to Mr. Bruce, who had begun to enumerate the class rules. By rule number four ("All hail the mighty whistle!"), Cordelia started to relax. *The boy's gone*, she thought. *There's nothing to be afraid of.*

A few minutes later, the sobbing began anew. Cordelia stiffened. "You hear that?" she whispered to Agnes.

"Hear what?"

"Crying."

Agnes listened intently for a few moments before finally shaking her head. The boy's cries grew in intensity. Cordelia scanned the bleachers. The other students were listening to Mr. Bruce with bored expressions.

They didn't hear the crying at all.

How is that possible? Cordelia wondered. *Why am I the only one who—*

Her eyes settled on Benji.

41

The boy shifted uncomfortably in his seat, glancing down with frightened eyes. He pulled the earbuds from around his neck and started to slip them into his ears, then noticed Mr. Bruce looking his way and twisted their cord between his fingers instead.

He wants to put them on to block out the crying, Cordelia thought. A smile spread across her face. *He hears the boy too!*

Cordelia wanted—no, *needed*—to talk to him. She had so many questions. Was this the first time he'd heard the ghost? Did he have any idea who the boy was? It wasn't exactly something you could bring up in the middle of gym class, however, so Cordelia was forced to wait through stretching exercises and an interminable kickball game before she could make her move. Finally, the bell rang. Cordelia ran up to Benji as he gathered his stuff from the bleachers. He was already wearing his earbuds.

"Hey," she said. "I'm Cordelia. Can we talk?"

Benji didn't even acknowledge that she had spoken. He ducked beneath his hood, wove past the departing students, and vanished around the corner.

5

A Brief Game of Soccer

It was impossible to pin Benji Núñez down and have an actual conversation. He was always the last student to arrive, usually after the teacher had already begun the lesson, and the first to leave, bursting from his seat the moment the bell rang. Cordelia had no idea where he ate lunch. She couldn't find him at recess. The boy was a master at avoiding people. Cordelia even tried following him from one class to the next, just to see why he was late. It turned out that Benji took the craziest, most convoluted path possible, stretching a two-minute walk into ten.

The boy made no sense.

While Benji Núñez remained a mystery, Cordelia

learned plenty about Agnes. Her family spent summers touring national parks, she had never seen an R-rated movie, and she wanted to be an environmental scientist when she grew up. The two girls eased into a comfortable friendship. They didn't have a lot in common, but they both needed a friend. Sometimes that was enough.

"What's Benji's deal, anyway?" Cordelia finally asked Agnes one day.

"You tell me," Agnes said with a knowing smile. "You're the one who stares at him all day long."

"That's not—" started Cordelia. "I don't *like* him. Not even as a friend. I'm just *curious.*"

"I'll tell you what I know," Agnes said, "but only if you walk faster. I don't want to be late."

"But it's math," Cordelia said with a grimace. "Hallway time good. Math time bad."

"Mrs. Machen is sweet."

"You just like her because she lets you use the Chromebook all period. You don't even have to pay attention!"

"It's not my fault that regular math is too easy for me!" Agnes exclaimed. "And working on those websites is not as great as it seems. It's kind of boring, and it makes the other kids really mad. Mason threw a gum wrapper in my hair yesterday, and even Kate Muloni laughed. I thought she was my friend."

"Kate Muloni walks like a penguin," Cordelia said. "Did you tell Mrs. Machen?"

"Ugh," Agnes said. "Everyone already thinks I'm the teacher's pet. That's the last thing I need."

Although Agnes was clearly the smartest kid in their grade, Cordelia didn't think she was any teacher's pet. In fact, she wasn't convinced that their teachers even *liked* Agnes. She wasn't easy-smart, like Aaron Weber, who spoke only when spoken to and got a hundred on every test. Instead, Agnes asked questions their teachers didn't understand and corrected them when they were wrong. When they sent Agnes off on her own to complete special enrichment assignments, Cordelia suspected they were doing it to get rid of her.

"Don't worry about what anyone else thinks," Cordelia said, giving Agnes a little hug. "They're just jealous because you're a genius."

"I guess," Agnes said.

"Now tell me about Benji."

"Which Benji? This year or last year?"

"Huh?"

"He was totally different last year," Agnes said. "Always smiling and talking. Popular, but not mean

45

popular like some other kids. He was really good at soccer, too. Helped win our town's travel team some big trophy."

"What happened?" Cordelia asked.

"I don't know," Agnes said. "All of a sudden Benji started missing a lot of school. He quit the soccer team. There were rumors that he was really sick. Then one time in science he just started screaming and screaming until the nurse had to come and get him. He was absent for a long time after that. People said he'd gone crazy." Agnes shrugged. "When he finally came back, it was a completely different Benji. Always off in his own world. The earbuds. The hood."

Benji must have seen the ghost for the first time last year, Cordelia thought. *That's why he freaked out.*

Cordelia knew exactly how he felt.

"Why are you so interested in Benji Núñez?" Agnes asked. "For real?"

"I guess I feel bad for him," Cordelia said, which wasn't exactly a lie. "He needs a friend. Trouble is, I can never seem to talk to him. He's a tough one to track down."

"I know he plays soccer behind the school during recess. Maybe you can talk to him there."

"Thanks, Ag," said Cordelia. "I'll give it a try."

They arrived at math. A few kids smiled at Cordelia or gave her a wave. Lily Chen asked her what she got for problem fourteen on the homework last night.

No one talked to Agnes at all.

It was a crisp autumn day, and Cordelia paused to zip up her new coat. A few sixth graders lounged in the wooded area, while the more athletically inclined played four square on the blacktop or soccer in the grassy field that adjoined the parking lot. She continued along the tree-lined path that led toward the back of the school, passing an empty playground on her right—popular with the fifth graders, who had recess the following period, but shunned by the older students. On the other side of a lonely swing set, Cordelia came to a wooden gate sandwiched between the wall that surrounded the school and the school itself. She could hear a distant *thwack* behind it.

She passed through the gate and found Benji kicking a soccer ball against the back wall.

Cordelia's knowledge of soccer began and ended with "get the ball in the net," but she could tell that he was really good. The ball made a whizzing noise as it sailed through the air, smacking the wall in the exact same spot over and over again.

Benji didn't look sullen when he was playing soccer. He looked relaxed. Happy. A typical sixth grader enjoying recess.

That all changed the moment she called out his name.

"What do you want?" he asked, picking up the soccer ball and cradling it protectively. "Why are you here?" He didn't just look annoyed; he looked distraught. Cordelia felt a pang of guilt. *This is his secret place, and I've ruined it.*

"I can see the ghost too," she said.

After an initial moment of genuine shock, Benji's expression quickly turned bewildered. It was almost convincing.

"No idea what you're talking about," he said, and started to walk away. This was too much for Cordelia. She had spent over a week trying to have one stupid conversation with this kid, and she wasn't going to let him escape so easily.

She ran in front of Benji and blocked his path.

"I know you heard the boy crying," Cordelia said, jabbing her finger in his face. "You might be able to hide it from everyone else, but not me!"

"Heard *who* crying?" Benji asked, scoffing. "A . . . ghost?"

He could barely bring himself to say the word.

"You're scared," Cordelia said. "It's okay! I'm scared too! But if we work together, we can—"

Benji slipped around her with a lightning-fast move that must have left defenders in the dust back on the soccer field. He headed toward the other side of the school, already yanking his earbuds from his pocket. Cordelia felt panic well up inside her.

I need to do something, she thought. *I might not get another chance to talk to him alone!*

"You stink at soccer!" she screamed.

This stopped Benji in his tracks, just like she'd hoped it would. In her experience, athletic boys always had the hugest egos.

"What did you say?" he asked, giving her his full attention now.

"I said you stink at soccer. That must be why you play back here all alone. Pure embarrassment."

"Just so you know," he said, coming a few steps closer. "I scored the most goals in our entire league last year."

"That was last year," Cordelia said. "Guess you stopped practicing. Or maybe"—she feigned a look of compassion—"you had some sort of serious injury? That could explain why your kicking is so pathetic."

Benji's cheeks flushed.

"My kicking is not pathetic."

"Prove it, then," Cordelia said, crossing her arms. "I'll stand up against that wall and play goalie. You kick it past me. Think you can do that?"

"In my sleep."

"In your dreams, maybe," Cordelia said. "You get it by me, I'll never talk to you again. In fact, I'll never even look in your direction. You have my word."

"I'm liking this plan."

"I stop the kick, though, and you have to tell me everything you know about the ghost in the gym."

She saw it again: the flicker of fear on Benji's face the moment she'd said *ghost*. That was good. She was counting on that fear for her plan to work.

"I told you," Benji said, "there is no—"

"Deal or no deal, Benji Núñez?" Cordelia asked. "If not, no worries. I'll be back tomorrow to ask again." She examined the area like a prospective homeowner. "I love this adorable little spot. I mean, I could see myself coming here. Every. Single. Day."

"Fine," Benji said through gritted teeth. "I'll tell you anything you want to know—*if* you block it. But that's not gonna happen."

They returned to the wall and agreed on the boundaries of the goal—a small pile of stones on one side, a long vertical crack on the other. Benji ran out to a spot about eight yards away. Cordelia windmilled her arms and jumped up and down like a boxer preparing for a fight. It seemed like something a goalie might do.

Benji gave her a strange look.

"You even *play* soccer?" he asked.

"That's funny," Cordelia said. "After seeing the way you kick, I was going to ask you the same question."

Benji slammed the ball into the grass and took a few steps back, preparing to take a running start.

Cordelia bent her knees and wiggled her fingers. *I have to time this perfectly. That's the only way it'll work.*

Benji ran forward, pumping his arms in smooth, fluid motions. He eyed the ball, lining up a masterful shot that would no doubt zip past her, and brought back his foot . . .

"*Ghost!*" Cordelia screamed, pointing behind him.

Benji let out a small moan of horror and whipped his torso around. His foot had already begun its forward momentum, however, and glanced off the side of the ball, sending a weak squib in Cordelia's direction.

She picked up the ball.

"Where is it?" Benji asked, looking desperately all around him while backing toward Cordelia. "Where's the ghost? I don't see it!"

He saw the ball in Cordelia's hands, and his face fell as realization set in. Instead of feeling victorious, Cordelia felt embarrassed. Her plan had worked, but it had been a cheap trick.

"Sorry," she said.

"Not cool," Benji agreed, but then he smiled slightly, as though he was a little impressed, too. She decided that Benji Núñez might not be so bad after all.

The recess bell rang.

"Time to go," Benji said.

"No way," Cordelia said, grabbing him by the elbow. "You have to tell me what you know! You promised!"

"I will," Benji replied with a solemn expression. "But now isn't the time. Can you meet me by the lockers after school today? I'll tell you what I know about the boy. The other ones too."

It took a moment for Benji's last words to register.

"What other ones?" Cordelia asked.

Ghost Tour

Cordelia arrived at the lockers just after three. Benji was already waiting for her, slouched down with one foot planted against the wall. There was a resolute expression on his face, as though talking to Cordelia was an unwelcome task that needed to be completed as quickly as possible. She tried not to take it personally.

"So what's the plan?" Cordelia asked.

"We walk around," Benji said. "I tell you things. Afterward, you never talk to me again."

Before Cordelia could reply, Benji started walking. She followed him.

Shadow School was even creepier at this time of day, when the classrooms were silent and no students roamed the halls. Occasionally, Cordelia and Benji passed a teacher hustling toward the parking lot. No one asked them where they were going. Cordelia suspected that the adults didn't like the silence of the building any more than she did.

"Could you always see ghosts?" she asked.

"Only in Shadow School. Never anywhere else."

"When did it start?" Cordelia asked. "What was the first ghost you—"

"I'll explain when we get there," Benji said.

"Get where?"

Benji ignored her and walked faster. An eggplant-colored runner stretched across the dark wooden floor of the hallway. Each door was bookended by an identical pair of tall stone planters. The plants inside them had died long ago.

They passed a teacher with teased hair and long dangly earrings. She was considering a blank bulletin board as though it were an exhibit in a museum.

"Some teachers are so hardcore about their bulletin boards," Cordelia whispered, trying to lighten the mood with small talk. "Like anyone actually looks at them."

Benji smiled, surprising her. Then he took a deep breath, like a swimmer about to start a race, and started to talk.

"I saw my first ghost last year," he said. "After soccer practice. Mr. Bruce—he's the coach—asked if I could toss the cones and some other equipment in the dungeon. That's what we call the room where all the sports stuff is stored. Mr. Bruce always asked me to put the equipment away. It's dark in there, and a lot of the other kids are too scared to go. There are all these stories. Things moving on their own, weird noises. But that didn't bother me. Back then, I wasn't scared of anything."

Benji's hood was down, but he toyed with the strings as he talked, as though he longed to duck back beneath his shell.

"What happened?" Cordelia asked.

"My hands were full, so I had to drop everything in order to open the door. It was dark inside. All I could see were shapes. Shoulder pads. Hockey sticks. Jocks aren't too good at putting their stuff away. I pulled on the string, and the lightbulb clicked on. In the back of the room there was a woman standing on one of the stepladders, looking through a shelf filled with catcher's masks and baseball mitts. She was wearing these old-fashioned clothes—a long skirt and this funny kind of hat. I said something stupid, like, 'Hey,' but the woman didn't say anything back. It was all so weird, but my mind didn't immediately scream 'ghost,' you know? I figured she was just someone's mom helping out, or maybe looking to see if her son's mitt got mixed up with the extra equipment. That happens. But when—"

They passed a bearded black man wearing a sweater vest. He was sitting at a table in a little lounge area, holding a newspaper only a few inches from his face. Unlike the other teachers, he seemed in no hurry to leave.

Cordelia started to wave, just to be polite, but Benji pushed down her arm.

"Don't bug him," he whispered. "He's trying to read."

Once they were past, Benji continued with his story.

"When I couldn't get the woman's attention, I started to get worried. I thought maybe she might be—I don't know, sick or something. That she might need help. So I got closer, and I tried to put my hand on her arm, only it passed right through. All I felt was—"

"Cold," Cordelia said. "Like sticking your hand in a bucket of ice."

Benji nodded.

"Yeah," he said. "That's exactly what it felt like."

Cordelia felt a sense of relief warm her body. Until this point, there had been a small part of her still worried that all this ghost stuff was in her head. Benji's detail about his hand erased any lingering concern. It was too specific to be a coincidence.

"What happened next?" Cordelia asked.

"What do you think happened? I freaked out! Just left all the equipment behind and ran. Mr. Bruce gave me an earful the next day."

"Is that why you quit soccer?"

"Nah," Benji said with a pained expression. "That came later. The woman in the dungeon was just the first. After that, I started to see ghosts everywhere."

"Wow," Cordelia said. "Guess I'm lucky. The only ghost I can see is the boy."

Benji laughed.

"What?" Cordelia asked.

"The man reading the newspaper. The woman looking at her bulletin board. Those were ghosts!"

Cordelia froze in place and fixed him with a dubious expression.

"They were *not*."

"That's why we walked this way," Benji said. "I wanted to make sure you could really see them. I told some kids on the soccer team what was going on last year, and they got mean about it. I had to make sure you were for real and not in on the joke."

"It was *a test*?" Cordelia asked. "You didn't think that getting so close to actual ghosts might be something I'd want to *know* first?"

"You've probably been even closer and not realized

it," Benji said. "Have you passed a woman who's always looking down at her cell phone? Near the front stairs."

Cordelia, remembering her first day of school, slowly nodded.

"How about a man looking out a window in a gray suit?"

Cordelia nodded again.

"Ghosts stay in one small area," Benji said. "A bench, like Newspaper Man. Or the gym, like the boy. There's a doctor wearing green scrubs who mostly sticks to a supply closet, but sometimes she rushes down the hallway with her hands up in the air. It always happens real quick, like she's just been called into surgery."

"I've seen her." Cordelia shivered with fear and just an inkling of embarrassment: *How did I not know?* "I thought she was a science teacher. I'm such a dumbhead."

"Nah," Benji said. "You're stubborn and bossy, but you seem to have your head on straight. I went through the same sort of stuff at the beginning. I think your brain makes all kinds of excuses for the things it can't understand."

Cordelia swallowed deeply before asking her next question. Her mouth was dry.

"Have you talked to any of them?"

Benji looked at her as if she was crazy.

"Why in the world would I do *that*?" he asked.

"Maybe they could explain why they're here."

"I don't need to know," Benji said. "Besides, it doesn't work that way. The ghosts don't talk."

"But we both heard the boy crying!"

"Yeah, they make sounds. Mostly crying, when they do, though there was one last year that giggled." He looked down and fiddled with the strings on his hoodie. "I didn't like that one. But they never talk."

This piece of information raised all sorts of other questions in Cordelia's head: *Can they understand what we say? Do they choose not to talk? Or is that something they can't do anymore?* Benji didn't look like he shared her curiosity. To him, the ghosts were just a problem that he wished would go away.

"How many are there?" Cordelia asked.

"The number's always changing. New ones arrive. Old ones fade away."

"Fade away? Like . . . die? But they're already—"

"I don't get it either," Benji said. "I just do everything I can to avoid them completely."

"That's why you're always late to class, isn't it?" Cordelia asked. "You walk out of your way to avoid all the ghosts! And you wear the earbuds so you can't hear them!"

"It makes it easier," Benji said with a sheepish look.

"I told my parents, thinking I could just transfer to the public school on the other side of town, but that's not how it works. I'm stuck here. The only other option is a private school. I know Mom and Dad would do that if I asked—they'd do anything for me and my sisters—but they're both working two jobs as it is. Paying for a private school would break them. So I told them I made it all up."

Cordelia suddenly felt very selfish. Here she was, whining nonstop about moving to New Hampshire because her dad had lost his job, while Benji had been facing horrors on a daily basis in order to keep his parents happy.

It made her like Benji a lot more—and herself a lot less.

"It'll be easier now that there's two of us," Cordelia said.

She expected him to shake his head and tell her to bug off, but instead Benji reached into his bookbag and pulled out a carefully folded piece of paper. He handed it to Cordelia.

"I made this for you," he said. "It's a map of the school. I marked the places to avoid with red circles."

Cordelia unfolded the map. There were a lot of red circles, especially in the upper floors.

"Things are always changing," Benji said, "but this

should be a good starting point. We can share information. Erase the ghosts that vanish. Give each other a heads-up on the new ones."

"I thought you never wanted to talk to me again after today," Cordelia said with a grin.

"Sorry about that," Benji replied, brushing back his hair. "I had to make sure you were legit first. But it's actually nice to talk about this with someone."

"I know what you mean."

They started back toward the front entrance. Cordelia had told her parents that she was staying after school for math help. Her dad would be coming to pick her up any minute.

"Are you sure nobody else knows about this?" Cordelia asked as they descended the stairs.

"Pretty sure," Benji said. "I don't know why we're the only ones who can see them. The important thing is to ignore them, Cordelia. Don't talk to them. Don't look in their direction."

"Why not?"

"If you ignore them, it's like they can't see you," Benji said. "But that changes once they catch you looking. They *notice* you."

Cordelia nodded, remembering her experience with the little boy. He hadn't responded to any of her questions at first. It was only after she tried to touch him that he reacted to her presence.

"What happens if you don't look away?" Cordelia asked.

"I don't know," Benji said in a trembling voice. "And I really don't want to find out."

Glasses

Now that Cordelia knew her school was inhabited by ghosts, she refused to go anywhere by herself. Even the idea of walking down a crowded hallway filled her with fear. She didn't know every single student who attended Shadow School. How could she be positive who was alive and who was dead? The only thing she could do was stick to the path on the map and walk with her eyes down.

As the weeks passed, however, a strange thing happened: Cordelia got tired of being scared. She looked up more often and risked walking by herself. One day, she even glanced at a ghost from the corner of her eye. It was a short man with red hair. Cordelia wondered why she had ever thought he was so scary. It was like a movie that was terrifying when you were a little kid but surprisingly tame when you revisited it later in life.

Suddenly, she was no longer scared.

She was curious.

Each ghost was a walking mystery. They might have been a little scary, but the questions they set off in Cordelia's head drowned out the *thump-thump-thump* of her racing heart.

Who were they when they were alive? How did they end up at Shadow School? Why are Benji and I the only ones who can see them?

Instead of avoiding the ghosts, Cordelia rearranged her walking routes in order to pass as many as possible. Each one seemed to exist in its own little world bordered by invisible walls. A wizened old man wearing a Detroit Tigers cap paced back and forth through the stacks of the library, his hands behind his back. A girl her own age sat at an empty desk, waiting for a class that would never begin. They weren't always in these "ghost zones," as Cordelia called them, but they were never anywhere else. Their actions repeated like a video loop. On the fourth floor, a young woman stared at herself in the bathroom mirror, puckering her lips and fixing her hair as though getting ready for a date. In the cafeteria kitchen, a heavyset man mimed the motions of baking a cake—pouring flour, cracking eggs, stirring, opening the oven door—then started the process anew.

One time, Cordelia stared too openly, and the cook took notice.

He carefully laid his invisible spoon on the table and started in her direction. Cordelia ran as fast as she could, only looking back when she was a safe distance away. The cook stood at the threshold of the kitchen, his palms flat against an invisible barrier. He was still watching her, but he had reached the border of his ghost zone and was unable to pursue her any farther.

He didn't look scary. He looked desperate.

A few days later, Cordelia hesitantly returned. The cook didn't register her presence at all, as though some kind of reset button had been pushed. Cordelia was relieved, but she also realized how lucky she had been.

What if the next ghost is faster? What if not all of them are nice?

After her experience with the cook, Cordelia went back to avoiding the ghosts. Curious or not, she knew she couldn't risk it.

Except for the boy.

Cordelia visited him every day, either in between periods or for a few minutes after school, before the buses left. She didn't go beneath the bleachers again. Instead, Cordelia sat by the opening with her body half-turned, watching the boy from the corner of her eye. In the beginning, he was always crying. But then Cordelia started to talk to him. She told him about her life in California and how much she still missed it. She talked about her teachers. Ms. Patel, who gave a lot of work but made science interesting; Mr. Derleth, who always knew some obscure fact or story that helped bring history to life; and Mrs. Machen, who made Michael Davies redo forty long division problems because he forgot a single decimal point.

As Cordelia talked, the boy's tears gradually subsided. He crept closer, his glasses askew on his face, and sat by the edge of the opening, listening to her. After a week of this, Cordelia finally risked making eye contact.

"Who are you?" she asked.

The boy gave her a blank stare. Cordelia wasn't sure he knew the answer any more than she did.

Halloween used to be Cordelia's favorite holiday, but without Ava and Mabel it didn't seem the same. She still might have gone trick-or-treating if Agnes had expressed any enthusiasm whatsoever, but after an incident with Mason James and a carton of eggs the previous year, Agnes had sworn off the holiday forever. In the end, Cordelia didn't even bother getting a costume.

Instead, she spent Halloween evening in front of her Chromebook, snacking on candy corn and researching ghosts. Usually she focused on the scary hauntings, but her experience with the boy had inspired her to take a different approach.

"Good spirits," she googled.

This took her to a list of stores that sold alcohol, so Cordelia refined her search.

"Good spirits dead," she typed, and then, after tossing a handful of candy corn in her mouth, added, "sad."

The first website she clicked on was a blog written by a husband-and-wife ghost-hunter team. They claimed that spirits had gotten a bad rap and were nothing like the bloodcurdling entities popularized by horror movies. The ghosts they had encountered during more than thirty years of experience were "lost, harmless travelers who had gotten stuck in a world they no longer belonged in."

Cordelia read the words over and over again, mouth agape.

Lost, harmless travelers . . .

It was like a river had been forded in her brain, allowing her access to startling new ideas. She considered all the spirits she had seen. The crying boy. The sad cook who couldn't follow her past the kitchen. The man in the gray suit, looking down at her from the window.

It all fit.

"They're not dangerous," Cordelia said. "They're trapped!"

Her fingers flew across the keyboard with renewed determination. *We should be helping them,* she thought, *not avoiding them.* Cordelia researched ways to help a ghost leave the "material realm" and move on to the next "plane of existence." She scanned blogs. She watched YouTube videos. She read posts on Reddit.

As far as Cordelia could tell, spirits might have trouble "moving on" for any number of reasons. In the movies it was always something dramatic, like wanting their murder to be avenged, but that wasn't necessarily the case with real-life hauntings. One recently deceased grandmother, for example, hung around the house for a few days to make sure her beloved cat found a new home. A penny-pinching husband haunted his wife until she stopped leaving the hallway light on at night. The owner of a muddy Mercedes wanted one last trip through the car wash. These particular ghosts reminded Cordelia of the ones at Shadow School. The cook trying to bake a cake. The woman looking at herself in the mirror. The teacher staring at the bulletin board. They each had something they wanted to accomplish. Nothing major. Just a normal part of life. And just like the other ghosts, they wouldn't be able to move on until . . .

68

It couldn't be that easy, could it?

Cordelia's mind jumped into overdrive, already forming a plan. She knew Benji would say it was too dangerous, but she had to try it, just to see what would happen.

Ten minutes later, her parents knocked on her door and said they were heading out for a few minutes to restock their candy supply. Cordelia surprised them by asking if she could come too.

There was something she needed to buy.

The next day, Cordelia made a lame excuse to Agnes and slipped out of the lunchroom. Benji was waiting for her by the lockers. He was wearing a brown hoodie today.

"You know," Cordelia said, "there are these things called shirts. They're like hoodies with buttons. You should check them out."

"It'll never catch on," Benji replied. "Why'd you want to meet?" He phrased his next question in a kind of code, in case any of the passing students happened to hear them. "Is there a new red circle to add to our map?"

"Even better," Cordelia said with a mischievous gleam in her eyes. "There's something I want to try."

"I don't like the sound of that."

Unlike Cordelia, Benji had no desire to learn more about the ghosts. He refused to even look in their direction, as though they were Medusas whose slightest gaze could turn him to stone.

"If you're thinking of going near one of them," Benji said, keeping his voice low, "count me out."

"You won't have to get close. I promise. I just want you to be there."

"Why?" Benji asked with a suspicious look.

"Um . . . you know," Cordelia said, not wanting to scare him away. "Just in case."

"In case something goes wrong!" Benji exclaimed. "Forget it! Listen, I know you think you're besties now with the one beneath the bleachers—"

"He *listens* to me."

"He's dead, Cordelia!" Benji exclaimed. "You shouldn't be messing around with them. This isn't a game." He flipped his hood over his head and started to walk away.

"What if I told you there might be a way to get rid of all the ghosts?" Cordelia asked.

Benji swung back around. There was a doubtful look in his eyes, but also the slightest bit of hope. "All the ghosts in the entire school?" he asked.

Cordelia nodded.

"I'm listening," Benji said.

"It's going to take more than that," Cordelia said. "Come on."

She led Benji to the spiral staircase on the west side of the building. As they ascended to the third floor, she explained her plan. Each ghost seemed trapped in a kind of loop. They were trying to perform a specific action—such as the cook baking a cake—but were unable to complete it. If Cordelia and Benji could help the ghost successfully perform whatever it was they were trying to do, then maybe the loop would be broken.

"What happens then?" Benji asked, looking closer to laughter than being convinced. "The ghost goes to heaven?"

"I don't know where they'll go," Cordelia said. "Somewhere different. Better. The important thing is they won't be trapped in Shadow School anymore."

"So the ghost of the old woman who walks back and forth across the stage, making a sweeping motion . . ."

"We give her a broom," Cordelia said, smiling. "Exactly! That's a good example."

"You're crazy!" Benji exclaimed. Cordelia opened her mouth to respond, but he added, "And before you tell me I don't know anything—I've done research too.

The dead move on when they feel at peace. Not because you hand them a broom!"

"That might be true in the real world," Cordelia said, "but if you haven't noticed, Shadow School works a little differently. You and I can see the dead! Is that normal? Maybe the ghosts here play by different rules too."

Benji grumbled unhappily, but it was clear that her point had struck home.

"I'll help you," he muttered. "But just this once."

The bearded man in the sweater vest was sitting at his usual table. As always, he held the newspaper far too close to his face. Cordelia casually took a seat across from him and pretended to check her phone. From the corner of her eye, she saw that the newspaper was the *Charlotte Observer* from June 12, 2002. The dead man squinted, clearly struggling to read the small print.

Cordelia took a deep breath in order to steady her nerves. Then she slid a pair of reading glasses across the table.

The man folded his newspaper down and stared in Cordelia's general direction, as though he had heard a strange sound outside and was looking through the window to investigate. He leaned forward, his face only inches from hers. Cordelia pretended she couldn't see him and continued to stare down at her phone, hoping the ghost wouldn't notice the bead of sweat that ran down her temple.

Finally, the man leaned back in his seat.

Cordelia shakily rose to her feet and crossed over to Benji, who looked as nervous as she felt. She risked a look over her shoulder and saw the bearded man slide the glasses over his ears.

"Whew," Cordelia whispered. "I was worried his hand would pass right through them."

The ghost looked down at the newspaper and burst into a glorious smile. He pushed the glasses up on his nose.

"It's working!" Cordelia said.

"What if they're not the right prescription?"

"I don't think it matters. It's just a symbol. The key that will let him leave."

The bearded man, now holding the newspaper a normal length away from his face, flipped to the next page and propped his feet up on the table. All the frustration left his body. He looked ten years younger.

A black triangle the size of a welcome mat appeared in the air above him, hovering a few inches below the ceiling.

"What's *that* thing?" Benji asked, taking a few steps back and pulling Cordelia along with him.

The triangle grew until it was half the size of the

room. It should have been terrifying. But looking at it, Cordelia felt only a sense of peace and joy. It slid open from the bottom, like a garage door, revealing a gentle, flickering light that brought to mind a cozy fireplace on a cold winter's night. The man began to rise upward, still reading his newspaper without a care in the world. A breeze kissed the back of Cordelia's neck and fluttered the papers of a nearby bulletin board. Lights flickered on and off. A vacuum that had been left behind by a careless custodian suddenly *vroomed* to life.

The man vanished into the light. The triangle closed again, faster than it had opened, and disappeared.

Cordelia turned to Benji, whose look of astonishment no doubt mirrored her own. *We freed him*, she started to say, but then she saw Agnes standing behind them, and the words got stuck in her throat.

"Hey," Cordelia said with a friendly wave.

Agnes pointed past them with a trembling finger. Her face was ashen.

"What was *that*?" she asked.

Cordelia burst into a huge grin and threw her arms around Agnes.

"This is so great!" she exclaimed. "You can see the ghosts too!"

"Ghosts?" Agnes asked, pulling away. "What ghosts?"

Cordelia stared at her, confused.

"You didn't see a man in a sweater vest?" she asked, spirits sinking.

"No."

"How about a giant hovering triangle?" Benji asked.

"No!" Agnes exclaimed. "And before you ask, I didn't see any dragons or leprechauns, either."

"Then what *did* you see?" Benji asked.

"The lights started flickering on and off. And things got windy all of a sudden. It was really weird."

Cordelia stopped to think. Despite her hopes to the contrary, Agnes didn't have the same special ability as they did. She could only see the way that supernatural phenomena affected things in the real world, like flickering lights.

"What are you doing here, anyway?" Benji asked. "Were you following us?"

Agnes's cheeks reddened.

"It's *your* fault," she exclaimed, jabbing her index finger in Benji's direction. "Ever since Cordelia started hanging out with you, she's been acting super strange. I wanted to see what was going on."

"I'm sorry," Cordelia said. "I should have told you."

"Told me *what*?"

Cordelia glanced at Benji, who gave a shrug. *She's seen so much. Might as well tell her the rest.*

"Shadow School is haunted by a slew of ghosts," Cordelia said, using a measured tone of voice in order to make her words sound as rational as possible. "And Benji and I are the only ones who can see them. They're trapped here for some reason. We don't know why. Or how. But we're trying to figure out how to help them."

"*She's* trying to figure out how to help them," Benji clarified. "I just want them to go away."

Cordelia expected Agnes to react with shock or horror. Maybe even anger that Cordelia had kept the truth from her for so long.

Instead, she looked relieved.

"I thought you didn't want to be friends anymore," she said, staring down at her clunky shoes. "Only you were too nice to tell me, so you were just going to ignore me until I took the hint. But ghosts?" She smiled wide, blue braces gleaming. "That's not so bad!"

"Of course I still want to be friends with you," Cordelia said, feeling terrible that Agnes had ever thought otherwise. She reached up and took the taller girl by the shoulders. "And now that you know the truth, the three of us can work together! Like a team! Right, Benj?"

Cordelia glared at him until he replied.

"Can't wait," he said, with two half-hearted thumbs-ups.

"There's one problem," Agnes said with a worried look. "Even if I believe you about the ghosts, it's like you said: you can see them; I can't." She looked disappointed in herself, as though she had done something wrong. "What can I possibly do to help?"

Cordelia grinned.

"I have an idea about that."

Confirmation

Cordelia stared out the window as they drove through downtown Ludlow. There were a few old pickup trucks parked in front of Lily's Breakfast Nook, but other than that the town was deserted. A banner strung from one side of the street to the other announced that the Ludlow Holiday Festival was only a few weeks away.

There was no traffic. There was never any traffic.

"Does Mrs. Machen always offer extra help this early?" Mr. Liu asked as they stopped at the only traffic light in town.

"Um, I'm not sure. I'll have to ask."

Cordelia turned away so her father couldn't see the

guilty expression on her face. She wasn't really going for math help (though she could certainly use it). That was just the lie she'd told her parents in order to get a ride to school. Cordelia wanted to prove that what had happened with Newspaper Man wasn't a fluke, which required getting into the building before the other students arrived.

"This is really nice of her," Mr. Liu said. "Not a lot of teachers would come to work early just to help their students."

"Yeah," Cordelia said. "Mrs. Machen's the best."

Mr. Liu gave her a strange look.

"Last week you said her classroom was the place 'where time stops and smiles die.'"

"She's really grown on me since then."

There were dark circles under her father's eyes. He had been on the phone with Cordelia's grandparents until after midnight again. She had overheard her father's end of the conversation through the bedroom wall. Her Chinese wasn't good enough to understand every word, but she got the main gist: Nainai and Yeye wanted them to move back to San Francisco, while her father insisted that Ludlow was their new home. It started out as a conversation and ended in an argument.

"I'm glad to see you taking an interest in your new school," Mr. Liu said as they left the downtown area and picked up speed. The sky above the distant mountains was streaked with lavender. "Your mother and I have been worried about you."

"I'm fine," she said.

"Have you made any new friends?"

My friends are in San Francisco, Cordelia started to say, and then stopped. Her grandparents had already made her father feel bad enough.

"A few," she said.

Mr. Liu smiled.

"That's great!" he said. "We'd love to meet them. You should invite them over."

"Maybe," Cordelia said as they pulled in front of Shadow School. Mr. Liu eyed the near-empty parking lot.

"You sure it's okay to drop you off this early?" he asked.

"Yup," Cordelia said, quickly slipping out the door before he could change his mind. "Thanks for the ride!"

The moment she entered the school, Cordelia heard raucous laughter in the main office. Students weren't allowed in the building so early—and she doubted a staff member would fall for her whole "math review" excuse—so she dashed down the hallway before anyone noticed she was there.

As Cordelia turned the first corner, she nearly collided with Dr. Roqueni.

"Sorry!" Cordelia exclaimed.

"No worries," Dr. Roqueni replied with a smile. Even this early in the morning she managed to look sleek and stylish, with a gray pencil skirt, navy blue blouse, and paisley-framed glasses. "You're here bright and early. Chorus rehearsal?"

Cordelia nodded, jumping at the ready-made excuse.

"Hmm," Dr. Roqueni said with a thoughtful expression. "But now that I think about it, chorus doesn't start for another twenty minutes."

"My dad had to drop me off extra early, so he could get to work on time," Cordelia said. That part, at least, was true. "I know students aren't supposed to be in the building this early, but it's freezing outside."

"Tell me about it," Dr. Roqueni said. "I've never gotten used to the weather here. I feel like I spend November through March in a constant state of shivering. How's this? I'll let you remain in the warmth, but in exchange you keep me company on my morning walk-through, at least until your rehearsal begins." She added, as way of explanation: "I like to check the building out before everyone arrives, make sure there's nothing that requires my immediate attention."

"Sounds great," Cordelia said. She liked the idea of hanging out with Dr. Roqueni, and there would still be plenty of time to perform her experiment before the other students arrived.

"It's hard to believe we're already two months into the school year," Dr. Roqueni said, walking at a rapid clip. Cordelia had to hustle to keep up. "How's Shadow School working out for you?"

"Good."

"Have you made any friends? I see you with Agnes Matheson a lot."

"Agnes is great."

"I'm glad to hear you say that," Dr. Roqueni said. "That girl can use a friend. You still miss sunny California?"

"Every day. Things were . . . simpler there."

"I feel you," Dr. Roqueni said with a wistful look. "Before I started working at Shadow School I was living in Paris. My favorite place in the world. I couldn't imagine ever leaving it."

"Why did you?"

"Family obligation," Dr. Roqueni said. "We don't always get to pick the life we lead, Cordelia. Sometimes it gets picked for us. You must understand that as well as anyone."

They continued to walk through the halls, talking about this and that. Just outside one of the language arts classrooms, Dr. Roqueni noticed an essay that had fallen from a bulletin board. She picked it up, nearly touching the foot of the ghost standing there, a young girl wearing a Little League uniform with *Bearcats* scrawled across the chest.

"Now where does this go?" Dr. Roqueni asked, oblivious to the girl.

Cordelia swallowed, doing her best to ignore the ghost.

"Over there," she suggested, pointing to a vacant spot on the board.

"Perfect," Dr. Roqueni said. She dug a pushpin out of her pocket and reattached the essay. "I'm telling you, half my job is keeping these bulletin boards up and running." She glanced down at her watch. "Thank you for keeping me company, Cordelia. Now I believe you have a chorus practice to get to."

"It was nice talking to you," Cordelia said, waving goodbye as she headed down the hallway.

"Cordelia?" Dr. Roqueni called after her. "The music room is the other way."

"Duh," Cordelia said, switching directions. "Sorry about that. Still learning how this school works, I guess."

Dr. Roqueni smiled.

"Don't worry," she said. "You'll get it eventually."

◆ ◆ ◆

After two flights of stairs and one wrong turn, Cordelia finally approached the woman staring at herself in the antique mirror. The electric sconces hadn't been switched on yet, so Cordelia had to make do with curtain-muffled sunlight. It was enough to see the intense look of frustration on the ghost's pale face, as though her own reflection was a puzzle she couldn't solve.

Cordelia pulled a makeup kit from her stuffed backpack.

It had been a gift from her aunt Eileen, a successful real estate agent who seemed impatient for her only niece to hit adolescence. The kit was still in its shrink wrap. Cordelia unwrapped it now and removed a tube of lipstick, which she rolled toward the woman in front of the mirror. The ghost glanced around with a confused look, as though she had heard her doorbell ring but found only an empty porch when she opened the door. She reached down for the lipstick. Her hand didn't pass through the silver tube, but she wasn't able to curl her fingers around it, either. It was as though her hands were frozen solid. The best she could do was nudge the lipstick with her fingers.

The woman huffed in annoyance and returned to studying her reflection.

It's close to what she needs, Cordelia thought. *But not exactly right.*

Cordelia tried an eyeliner pencil, with the same result, then a bottle of pink nail polish. This time, the ghost's hand passed right through it. Her lips tightened, as though she suspected someone was playing a cruel trick on her, and she took a few angry steps toward Cordelia.

The nail polish is completely wrong, Cordelia thought. *Getting colder.*

She stood perfectly still and forced herself to look away until the moment passed. Once the woman returned to studying her reflection, Cordelia decided to give it one more try. She got as close as she dared and slid a blush compact across the floor. The ghost smiled with delight and snatched it up as deftly as any living person. She removed the brush and instantly started applying it to her ashen cheeks.

Duh, Cordelia thought. *She's so pale. Of course blush is what she would want first. I have to be more observant.*

The black triangle appeared a few moments later. When the door slid open this time, it wasn't firelight that filled the room but the bright, pulsating lights of a party. While Newspaper Man's lights had been warm and peaceful, perfect for reading a leather-bound book on a snowy winter evening, these lights promised dancing and excitement. Cordelia thought she might have even heard a thumping bass line in the distance.

They're going to different places, Cordelia thought.

The woman floated upward and vanished. There was so much that Cordelia still didn't understand, but one thing was for certain: Newspaper Man hadn't been a fluke. She had figured out how to help the ghosts.

"Who's next?" she asked.

Brightkeys

The three children met behind the school during recess. Benji didn't like missing his soccer time, but Agnes attended a gifted-and-talented program at the local college after school and couldn't stay past dismissal. Besides, Cordelia didn't want to wait that long to tell them the good news about Blush Lady. The moment they were alone, she relayed the morning's events in a rush of triumph. She expected congratulatory words and high fives, perhaps a brief smattering of applause.

Instead, her friends stared at her with marked disapproval.

"You shouldn't have done that," Benji said, kneeing

his soccer ball into the air. "It was way too dangerous."

"I agree," Agnes said. "There's so much about these ghosts we don't understand. What if the woman had attacked you when you didn't give her the correct item?"

Benji nodded.

"We need to make decisions as a group from now on," he said.

Cordelia looked from Benji to Agnes with disbelief.

"Well, I'm glad you two are getting along," she mumbled.

Cordelia exhaled a plume of cold air and pulled her woolen hat over her ears. It wasn't even Thanksgiving yet, and the temperature had already dropped below anything she had ever experienced. She was bundled up with a winter coat, a scarf, and gloves. Agnes was wearing a light jacket. Benji was wearing shorts.

There's something wrong with them, Cordelia thought, shivering.

"What's done is done," Agnes said. "And trying to free another ghost was definitely the next logical step. In an experiment, you always test your hypothesis multiple times to make sure your conclusion is correct."

"What did we learn, exactly?" Benji asked while juggling the soccer ball with alternating feet. "Each ghost needs a special object in order to send them into—whatever waits for them past the triangle?"

"I think it's a different place for each ghost," Cordelia said. "Whatever makes them happy. The man with the newspaper wanted a quiet place to read. The woman wanted somewhere fun and exciting." Cordelia smiled, the name coming to her all at once. "The triangle takes them to their bright place. Or just . . . Bright. That's catchier."

"I like that," Benji said. "As long as we're naming things, what about the objects that send these ghosts along their way? We'll need a special name for those as well."

They debated it for a while. Agnes favored GFOs— "ghost-freeing objects"—but Cordelia and Benji thought that sounded like a standardized test. Since the objects unlocked the Bright, Cordelia suggested "keys" instead, which Benji amended to "Brightkeys." The moment he said it, the three friends knew they had found their winner.

Agnes clapped her hands together. "This is so much fun!" she exclaimed. "Naming things is important. It's another way to stay organized. I'll add a column marked 'Brightkeys' to the table I made on Google Docs."

"You made a table?" Cordelia asked.

"The most important part of any long-term experiment is staying organized from the get-go," Agnes said with a serious look. "I'll share the doc with both of you, so you can add information as you gather it. There's a row for each ghost, along with the most important data points: location, clothing, age, physical appearance, observable actions. Judging from our first two test cases, these spirits are definitely trying to drop as many hints as possible about their Brightkeys. A man with a newspaper needs glasses. A woman looking in the mirror needs makeup. Pretty obvious."

"They're looking for help," Cordelia said. "Like a shipwrecked sailor lighting flares and waving his arms back and forth."

"Or maybe it's not in their control at all," Benji suggested. "Maybe someone's trying to help them, like a guardian angel."

"Do you think all the Brightkeys will be as easy to figure out as the first two?" Agnes asked.

Cordelia and Benji shook their heads in unison.

"The man in the gray suit is just looking out the window," Benji said. "That's not much to go on. He could want anything."

"Same thing with the boy in the gym," Cordelia added. "He's wearing pajamas, which gives me some ideas, but I'd have to try them out to be sure."

Cordelia caught Agnes looking at them with a twinge of envy in her eyes, as though they were describing a party to which she hadn't been invited. *She can't see the ghosts*, Cordelia reminded herself. *We have to be careful what we say so she doesn't feel left out.*

"You think this will work for every ghost?" Cordelia asked Agnes, tossing her a question so she could be included. "Do they all have Brightkeys?"

"Let's assume so until we learn otherwise," Agnes said. "It's just a matter of figuring it out. That's why you need to be as detailed as possible when you describe them." She looked down. "That's the only way I'll be able to help you."

"I could try drawing them," Cordelia suggested.

"Great," Agnes said. "You do that, and Benji can fill out the table."

"There's *homework* now?" Benji asked. "These ghosts are the worst."

"Sorry," Agnes said. "Cordelia told me I was in charge of 'figuring stuff out.' And if we really want to understand what's going on, we need to gather as much information as possible. That's the only way we'll see if there are any patterns to all this."

"I think it's an amazing idea," Cordelia said.

Agnes blushed.

"One more thing," she said. "One of you mentioned that certain ghosts are opaque while others are translucent?"

"Wasn't me," Benji replied. "I don't even know what those words mean."

"You can see through some ghosts, but not all of them."

"Oh," Benji said. "That was me. Yeah, the ghosts tend to gradually disappear for some reason. Like the girl on the third floor, wearing the bicycle helmet? She's faded a little since September. And when I came back after the summer there were a few ghosts that were completely gone."

"That's good, right?" Cordelia asked. "That means they escaped on their own."

"I'm not sure," Benji said. "Newspaper Man went to a good place. You could feel it when he passed through the triangle. The ghosts that disappear, though—they don't seem so happy about it. Almost like they're sick." He threw his hands into the air. "But that doesn't make sense, right? How can a dead person get sick?"

"It's useless trying to draw any conclusions yet," Agnes said. "We need more specific data first. Let's use a scale to identify each ghost's stage of visibility, so we can see which ones are getting close to the end. Something simple. How about one to three, with one being they look like you and me, and three being they're almost invisible."

"We should probably focus on helping the threes

first," Cordelia said. "Since they're the closest to disappearing completely."

Agnes nodded. "I'll add a column to the table," she said.

"More homework," Benji muttered.

"Stop whining," Cordelia said. "We're the only ones who can help these poor people. We *have* to."

Benji's expression turned solemn. "I know," he said.

A silence settled over the group as they pondered the sheer responsibility of this new undertaking. This wasn't like finishing a book report by its due date or remembering to put your yogurt container in the recycling bin.

We can't mess this up. It's too important.

Cordelia wished there was a grown-up who could tell them whether or not they were doing things the right way. *Maybe I should try my parents again. Or Dr. Roqueni.* More than likely, the principal wouldn't believe them. It might be even worse if she did; the adults would immediately take over, and the children would be ushered away "for their own good." Cordelia didn't want that. All this ghost stuff was overwhelming and terrifying, but for the first time, she felt excited about her new life.

Lunch

In the next few weeks, they freed eight more ghosts.

Sometimes, the Brightkey was hard to miss. The old woman making sweeping motions in the auditorium really did need a broom; the moment she touched the one Cordelia left her, a black triangle snapped into existence, spreading golden shafts of sunlight across the stage. Other Brightkeys required a sharper eye but were still fairly obvious. A young girl haunting a third-floor supply closet wore a backpack festooned with stuffed elephants, and after noticing a plastic clasp where another one used to hang, Cordelia left a replacement. The girl smiled with delight and added it to her collection. Her Bright was the greenish-yellow of African grasslands.

Cordelia and her friends celebrated each time they freed a ghost, usually with ice cream sandwiches purchased from the cafeteria vending machine. Their happiness came in different hues. Benji felt a calming relief knowing that there was one less ghost to pass in the halls. Agnes experienced the intellectual satisfaction of successfully solving a puzzle. Cordelia's happiness was the strongest of all, perhaps because it was such a new experience: the pure joy of having done something good without expecting anything in return.

Unfortunately, it wasn't always that easy.

Some ghosts revealed no obvious clues about their Brightkeys. The man in the gray suit. A teenager with a sullen expression sitting on the floor of the main office. A tall woman taking a nap.

What do they need? Cordelia wondered, staring up at her ceiling during sleepless nights. *How can I help them?*

The group's successes brought Cordelia a brief feeling of elation, but their failures could plunge her into a bad mood for days.

They cataloged all the ghosts according to Agnes's visibility scale and tried to focus as best they could on the threes, those that seemed closest to leaving the world forever. One of them was a high school girl who was difficult to see unless you already knew she was there, like a constellation in the night sky. Since she was wearing shorts and sunglasses, they figured that maybe the girl's Brightkey would be something from the beach. The kids ransacked their own possessions— something they were doing quite often these days—and left the girl a half-used tube of sunscreen, a bathing suit, and a towel. Her hand passed through the sunscreen, not even nudging it the slightest bit with her ghostly fingers. She ignored the other two items altogether.

At the time, Cordelia didn't feel particularly dis-suaded. They rarely nailed the Brightkey on the first attempt. She was certain they would figure out a better approach once they had a chance to brainstorm.

The next day, the girl was gone.

Cordelia had no idea what that meant, exactly. *Gone.* But it was far different from when the ghosts passed into the Bright. To Cordelia, it felt as though the girl had died all over again. Except this time, it was her fault.

When Cordelia and her dad drove to school one mid-December morning, there was a thin layer of snow on the ground.

"So how are things going with Mrs. Machen?" Mr. Liu asked. "You've been getting a lot of extra help recently, but your grades don't seem to be improving."

Cordelia was glad her dad was so focused on the road. Otherwise he might have seen the panicked look that flashed across her face.

"It's helping a lot," she said. "I know my grades still aren't great, but without the extra help I'd probably be failing completely."

"Maybe we should set up a conference with your teacher to talk about it."

"No," Cordelia said, a hair too fast. "That's okay. I've got it under control."

Mr. Liu glanced over at her. Cordelia wondered if she saw a hint of suspicion in his eyes or if she was just being paranoid.

"Okay," he said. "We'll give it a little more time." He tapped the steering wheel in rhythm to the music playing softly on the radio. "How are your friends doing? I haven't asked you in a while."

"They're fine," Cordelia said. "Actually, lunch yesterday was pretty funny. Benji ate a whole plate of spaghetti with a spoon, just to prove that he could do it. Me and Agnes couldn't stop laughing."

Mr. Liu smiled to himself.

"I meant your friends in California," he said.

"Oh. They're fine too, I guess."

Mr. Liu dropped her off at the curb. Cordelia

entered the school, pausing to stomp the snow off her boots, and went straight to the gym. The boy's crying stopped the moment she flicked on the lights. He came to the edge of the open bleachers, waiting for her with a smile on his face.

"Good morning," Cordelia said. She slid her book-bag off her shoulder and pulled out a wooden train whistle. "Let's try this today."

Despite her daily attempts, Cordelia had gotten no closer to discovering the boy's Brightkey. Her first idea had been a tissue for his tears. When that hadn't worked, she'd considered the fact that he was wearing pajamas—which seemed like an obvious clue—and changed her focus to bedtime items. In the following weeks, Cordelia had tried a glass of milk, a cup of water, a blanket, a pillow, three different kinds of nightlights, a toothbrush, toothpaste, and floss.

Nothing had worked.

The wooden whistle was the latest in a series of train-themed Brightkeys, including toy trains, stuffed trains, train tracks, and a conductor's hat. Cordelia placed the whistle at the boy's feet and watched anxiously as he bent down to grab it. *Come on*, she thought, clenching her hands tightly together. *Come on!*

His hand passed right through the whistle.

Other ghosts often grew upset at these failed

attempts, but the boy clapped his hands in delight, as if he and Cordelia were playing some sort of game.

"I thought for sure that would work," Cordelia said, stuffing the useless whistle back in her bag. She looked the boy over, wondering what she should try tomorrow, and noticed a new detail on his T-shirt: four black lines that crossed the locomotive at a slight angle. *That's weird*, Cordelia thought. *It looks like someone drew over his shirt with marker.* She wondered if the marks had always been there, or if she had just never noticed them before; the lines were very thin. *It probably doesn't mean anything,* she thought. *What about the glasses? Don't you usually take them off when you go to bed? Maybe that means he's leaving them on so he can see the pictures in a book—his Brightkey might be a bedtime story!*

While Cordelia wondered how many train books she could find at the public library, the boy took a seat at the edge of his ghost zone and crossed his legs like a kindergarten student at circle time. He gazed expectantly at Cordelia with his bespectacled eyes, waiting for her to talk to him as she did each day.

"Don't worry," Cordelia said, with confidence she didn't feel. "It's only a matter of time before we figure out your Brightkey. We're getting better and better. Just yesterday, we freed a man in the faculty bathroom upstairs. He wanted a cap to hide his bald spot."

The boy covered his mouth and rocked back and forth in silent laughter. Cordelia grinned. During times like this it was easy to forget that the boy was a ghost at all. Since his visibility level was only one, he looked no different from a living child.

That'll change if I can't figure out his Brightkey, Cordelia thought.

"Listen," she said, the smile vanishing from her lips. "I have some bad news. I might not be able to come here as often."

The boy pouted and crossed his arms. Cordelia held out an open hand.

"It's not that I don't *want* to," she said. "But I think my parents are starting to catch on that I'm not coming to school for extra math help. If they figure out the truth, I won't be allowed to come at all."

The boy nodded with a serious expression. Although he couldn't reply, Cordelia knew he understood everything she said. She wasn't sure why he was different from the other ghosts, who often seemed confused and frustrated by her presence. Cordelia believed that the boy's growing ability to communicate had something to do with the amount of time she spent with him—that she had, in some way or another, woken him up.

Sometimes, in the darkest hours of the night, she wondered how he had died. Had he been ill? Or had there been some sort of accident? In the end, she always ended up crying and feeling stupid for even thinking about it in the first place. What was the point? She couldn't change what had happened. There was only one way she could help him now.

"I wish I knew your name," Cordelia said.

The boy nodded: *I wish I could remember it.*

Even Cordelia had to admit that the lunchroom at Shadow School was pretty cool. It used to be a ballroom, back when the building had been used as a home and not a school. A giant chandelier hung from the cathedral ceiling, and the scuffs and scratches on the wooden floor only accentuated its natural beauty. Floor-to-ceiling windows lined the walls, revealing hallways on three sides and a stunning view of the White Mountains on the fourth.

Given the room's grandiose appearance, Cordelia had hoped that the food would be something special; alas, it was no better than her old school. In this one way, Shadow School and Ridgewood were precisely, depressingly equal.

"Look at this thing," Cordelia said, poking her

lasagna. "The noodles are all mushy and overcooked, but half the cheese is still unmelted. I don't even know how that's possible."

"You boil the noodles before you put it all together," Benji said. "They must have overcooked them, then they didn't bake the lasagna long enough to melt the cheese."

Cordelia and Agnes glanced across the table in surprise.

"You can cook?" Agnes asked.

"I have to take care of my little sisters when my parents work late," Benji said. "So yeah, sometimes I make dinner. Nothing fancy. Spaghetti, tacos—things like that. I've made lasagna a couple times. It's pretty good, but it takes forever."

"Shouldn't your parents hire a babysitter or something?" Agnes asked. "I mean, technically you're too young to—"

Benji waved the thought away.

"What are they going to do? Pay some high school student ten dollars an hour just to sit on the couch and text her boyfriend? There's no need for them to waste their money. I got it."

Cordelia forced down a bite of her lasagna, feeling guilty. She never cooked, unless you counted microwave popcorn. She had no responsibilities, no chores.

And yet all she had done since the move was complain.

"I wish I had a little sister," Agnes said. She had an older half brother from her father's first marriage, but he lived in Boston with his mom. "That must be so much fun."

"Hmm," Benji said, picking a soggy fry off Cordelia's plate. "I don't know if 'fun' is the word I'd use. How about . . . 'exhausting'? I actually fell asleep on the couch last week like an old man. And Sofia—"

"The six-year-old?" Cordelia asked.

"The twins are six," Benji said. "Sofia's eight, and she's the real troublemaker in the family. Anyway, she sneaks up while I'm sleeping and—" He paused, reconsidering. "I don't know if I should tell you this."

"You can't stop now!" Cordelia exclaimed.

"Fine," Benji said. "While I was sleeping, Sofia painted my fingernails with this glittery nail polish. Neon pink."

Cordelia and Agnes broke into laughter.

"Stop it," Benji said, though he was smiling himself. "It took me all night to get that stuff off. I had to scrub and scrub with soap and water. I have no idea how you girls do it."

"Um . . . nail polish remover?" Cordelia asked.

Benji's face fell.

"That's a thing?" he asked.

Agnes's laughter, which had already been pretty loud, now rose into a series of snorts—which made the three of them laugh even harder. Other students turned in their direction. Mrs. Machen, who was on lunch duty that day, gave them a withering gaze and placed a finger to her lips.

All of a sudden, Agnes stopped laughing and turned bright red. At first, Cordelia had no idea why. Then she saw Mason staring in Agnes's direction while making snorting, pig-like noises. His friends laughed hysterically.

"Ignore him," Cordelia said. "He's a jerk."

"I'll make him stop," Benji said.

He rose from the table with a dark look in his eyes, like he was about to do some kind of stupid boy thing that would only get him in trouble.

"Don't bother," Agnes said, straightening. "Cord's right. It's not worth it." She smiled with a hint of color in her cheeks. "But thanks anyway."

Benji settled back into his seat.

"I can't believe I used to be friends with that guy," he said. "Back when I was on the soccer team, we—"

Someone screamed.

The lunchroom fell quiet. All eyes turned to a red-headed girl. She was standing at her seat, staring down in astonishment at the chocolate milk splattered across the front of her shirt.

"Who threw that?" the girl screeched.

"It was my milk," said a boy from another table. His face was pale. "But I didn't throw it. Really. It just . . . it just . . ."

Mason, always the first to find the humor in someone else's misfortune, started to laugh. It was high-pitched and cruel.

He stopped immediately when a plate of lasagna smacked him in the face.

"Hey!" he exclaimed. A piece of stringy cheese dangled from his nose as he searched the lunchroom for the culprit, murder in his eyes. *"Who did that?"*

What followed was chaos.

Trays flew through the air, raining down lasagna, pizza, bagels, fries, sticky beverages, and the occasional healthy salad. There were no hurricane-force gales, no apparent cause for the objects to be moving on their own.

They simply moved.

What's happening? Cordelia thought.

A stampede of sixth graders attempted to flee the cafeteria, pushing and shoving their way through the double doors and creating a dangerous bottleneck. Mrs. Machen tried to maintain order, swatting away an obstinate slice of pizza like an annoying fly, but there was little she could do. Grant Thompson was knocked to the ground. Cordelia quickly helped him to his feet. His hair was matted with juice and there were tears in his eyes, as though his pets were dying all over again.

"Watch out!" Benji screamed.

The table next to Cordelia was rumbling like a volcano about to erupt. She pulled Grant to safety as it slid across the room, right where they had been standing a moment beforehand. The table flipped over and crashed through one of the interior windows, ending up in the hallway.

"Thanks," Grant said, and ran out of the cafeteria.

Cordelia joined Agnes and Benji, and together they helped a few other kids who had slipped on the floor or refused to come out of their hiding spots beneath the tables. Food and the occasional tray pummeled them from all directions. By the time they managed to get everyone to safety, the trio looked like they had just climbed out of a dumpster.

Dr. Roqueni entered the lunchroom. She was wearing a pristine white blouse. Cordelia suspected she might regret that decision very soon.

"You three need to get out of here," she said. "Now."

Cordelia thought she might have a point. Although the storm of food had begun to die down, the chandelier was now swinging back and forth like it was being ridden by a pack of invisible monkeys. Its moorings creaked and strained against the unexpected movement. Cordelia and her friends backed through the main door into a crowd of onlookers. Mr. Ward was standing guard, using his large frame and frightening scowl to keep the more curious students at bay.

Cordelia peeked past him. As the chandelier finally creaked to a stop, she glimpsed a strange figure standing in the far corner of the cafeteria. He was wearing suspenders over a linen shirt and black-tinted goggles that hid his eyes.

Ghost, Cordelia thought.

The man's gaze settled on her, and a look of surprise flitted across his features. Cordelia looked away, her instincts screaming that she didn't want this particular ghost to know that she could see him.

"Benji," Cordelia whispered. "You see that ghost in the corner of the lunchroom? Take a quick look, don't make it obvious."

Benji did as she asked, but it was already too late. The ghost had vanished.

The sixth graders were given a chance to clean up as best they could and then ushered into the auditorium. Dr. Roqueni stood on the stage, waiting for them to take their seats. Her lips were pursed with barely suppressed anger.

"In all my years as the principal of Shadow School, I've never seen such behavior," she said in a cold, quiet voice. "Throwing food at one another like *animals*! Pushing tables! It's a miracle that no one was hurt."

A few students protested their innocence, but not as many as Cordelia expected. Most were looking down at their laps as if it really had been their fault. *How could they think it was just a food fight?* Cordelia wondered. *They were there! They saw what happened!* Then again, things had been so chaotic. She imagined it would be easy, afterward, to assume that it had been a bunch of other students throwing food at one another. She remembered what Benji had said about the brain making excuses for the things it couldn't understand.

After threatening to cancel all field trips if anything like this ever happened again, Dr. Roqueni finally dismissed them. The students silently shuffled out of the auditorium while some of the adults formed a half circle around Dr. Roqueni: Mr. Derleth, Mr. Bruce (sporting a Kansas City Royals jersey), Mrs. Machen, and Mr. Ward. The custodian was wearing a tool belt with the biggest hammer that Cordelia had ever seen.

"What do you think they're talking about?" she asked.

"I know a way we can find out," Benji said. "Come on."

Cordelia and Agnes followed him down the hallway and into a narrow storage room behind the auditorium. They kept the lights off and felt their way between two hanging racks of dusty dresses and animal costumes. Benji opened a second door at the end of the room, and they emerged backstage. The curtains were drawn. Cordelia crept across the stage, wincing at every squeak in the floorboards, and peeked through the narrow opening between the curtains. The teachers were right on the other side, still in the midst of their hushed conversation.

". . . don't know why we're still talking about this," Dr. Roqueni said. "It was just some preadolescent nonsense. Even good kids have bad days."

"With all due respect," Mrs. Machen said, "you weren't there. I saw a carton of milk launch itself across the room and a table move without anyone touching it at all."

"I'm sure that's what you *thought* you saw," Dr. Roqueni said in a calming voice. "But we both know that simply isn't possible. Kids being kids. It's the only explanation."

"Or it could be starting again," Mr. Bruce said.

Until this point, Mr. Derleth had been listening with half-closed eyes, looking almost asleep. Now he gazed at Mr. Bruce with intense interest.

"What could be starting again?" he asked.

Cordelia remembered that Mr. Derleth was new, which meant he wouldn't know about events that had transpired before his tenure at Shadow School. The rest of the group shared questioning looks: *Do we tell him?*

"If you must know," Dr. Roqueni finally said, "something similar happened in the lunchroom about ten years ago. More childish nonsense. And then, a few weeks later, there was an incident in an eighth-grade science classroom. The students claimed that lab equipment was flying around the room on its own, but we all know that's impossible."

"Three students had to get stitches," Mr. Bruce said.

"Unfortunate," Dr. Roqueni said. "But that doesn't prove—"

"For a while, things went back to normal," Mrs. Machen said. "We thought it was all over. But then, just before summer vacation, a custodian named David Fisher was working late one night, and he just . . . vanished. No one has seen him since."

"That's horrible," Mr. Derleth said. "But what exactly are you suggesting? That there's something supernatural going on here?"

"The school's haunted," Mrs. Machen whispered.

Mr. Ward barked a laugh. "Come on," he said.

"It's true!"

"You telling me you've actually seen a ghost?"

"Well, not exactly," Mrs. Machen said, growing flustered. "It's more like a feeling."

Mr. Ward rolled his eyes.

"I know exactly what she's talking about," Mr. Bruce said, coming to the math teacher's defense. "I haven't seen anything either, but you couldn't pay me enough to stay in this school after dark. There's something off about this place. You can feel it."

"I should have taken that job at Chatham Prep," Mrs. Machen muttered. "They have a top-of-the-line copy machine there. I saw pictures of it on Facebook. It can make a hundred packets in less than three minutes!"

"I don't know what happened to poor Mr. Fisher," said Dr. Roqueni, "but I'm certain that there is a perfectly rational explanation for everything, including what happened in the lunchroom today." She checked her phone. "Now, I believe you all have classes to teach. Please keep these rumors to yourself. We don't want the children thinking that Shadow School is full of ghosts."

11

Agnes Makes a Fish Analogy

"Mom?" Cordelia called out, checking the contents of their pantry. "Do we have any chips?"

Mrs. Liu sat at the kitchen counter typing away at her laptop. She was wearing glasses, and her blond hair was tied in a bun. Work mode.

"There's hummus and carrots in the fridge," she said, half listening.

"These are my people friends," Cordelia said. "My rabbit friends don't come over until next week."

"Don't be smart."

"Sorry," Cordelia said, knowing that she got snappy when she was nervous. It was the first time she'd had guests in the house, and she wanted everything to go right. "I remember there being pretzels at some point."

"Your dad already ate them."

"Goldfish?" Cordelia asked, growing desperate now. "Cookies? Popcorn?"

"Check the top shelf. That's where I hide all the junk food."

Cordelia pulled over a stool and, after some digging and shifting, finally found a box of crackers. She fanned a row of them along the edge of a plate, then added hummus, carrots, grapes, and a spoonful of peanut butter.

Mrs. Liu finished typing something with a flurry of keystrokes and looked up. "It's nice to finally meet your friends," she said. "Agnes is . . . interesting. And obviously very intelligent." Mrs. Liu grinned and raised her eyebrows. "Benji's really cute."

"Stop," Cordelia said, reddening.

"I'm just making a casual observation. What are you guys up to down there?"

"Homework and stuff."

"Well, I'm glad you're finally settling in," she said, her eyes returning to the screen. "I know this place isn't as exciting as San Francisco, but there's something to be said for a calm, relaxing life. It just feels safer here."

Cordelia thought of a dozen replies to this, each more sarcastic than the last, and finally decided to just kiss her mom on the cheek instead.

She carried the snack plate downstairs to a rec room with books, board games, and an old Wii U console that Cordelia never used. Benji and Agnes were sitting at opposite ends of the couch. For the most part they got along okay, but that was when Cordelia was there to bridge their friendship. They normally didn't spend any time alone.

"Dig in," Cordelia said, placing the snack plate on the coffee table.

Agnes eagerly swiped a carrot through the hummus. Benji, looking somewhat disappointed by the choices, halfheartedly picked at the grapes.

"This is so fancy!" Agnes said. "I should have chipped in and made some brownies!"

"Seriously," Benji said.

"You're welcome," Cordelia said, glaring at Benji before turning to Agnes with a smile. "You can make brownies next time if you want."

"Next time?" Agnes asked.

"Yeah," Cordelia said. "I mean, this isn't the only time you're ever coming to my house."

Agnes beamed like a kid who'd just been given an open pass to Disney World. *After all this time, she still can't believe we're really friends,* Cordelia thought, disappointed in herself for not being a better one. She wasn't as popular at Shadow School as she had been at Ridgewood, but Cordelia had managed to strike up a few passing friendships with other kids in their class. Agnes, however, remained an outsider, awkwardly hovering at the edge of conversations even when Cordelia tried to include her.

I have to do a better job. The dead aren't the only ones who could use some help.

"I thought it would be easier if we met at my house," Cordelia said. "It's so hard to talk at school."

"Especially with all the food flying around," Benji said.

"Yeah," said Cordelia, leaning back in the couch. "So . . . what the heck *was* that? I assume it's somehow connected to the ghosts—because what else could it be?—but none of the other ghosts can make things fly through the air."

Agnes raised her hand.

"We're in my basement," Cordelia said, "not school. You can just talk."

"I think the man you saw at the back of the lunchroom was a poltergeist," she said.

"Isn't that just another word for a ghost?" Benji asked.

"Not exactly," Agnes said. "It's a special kind of ghost that can move objects around. The term actually originates in Germany, where there was a—"

"Okay," Cordelia said. "That certainly fits. But we're in the lunchroom every day. If that's his ghost zone, then why haven't we seen him before?"

"Maybe it works differently for poltergeists," Agnes suggested. "He might not have a ghost zone."

"You mean he can go wherever he wants?" Benji asked. "I don't like the sound of that."

"It's just a theory," Agnes said.

"And a good one," replied Cordelia, "but it doesn't tell us why he decided to let loose with the poltergeisting in a crowded room. The other ghosts we've seen want nothing to do with people at all."

"I'm not sure that's even a choice," Benji said, picking up another handful of grapes. "I don't think the ghosts are ignoring people on purpose. They can barely see us. Every so often someone will laugh really loud or drop something, and then a ghost might glance in their direction, but other than that, it's like we're invisible."

"What if someone walks through a ghost accidentally?" Agnes asked. "Someone like me who can't see them?"

Benji and Cordelia shared a quick smile.

"What?" Agnes asked.

"You did it yourself last week," Cordelia said. "Walked right through the mailman on the second floor. Then you just kind of wrapped your arms around

116

yourself and said, 'The school's chilly today.'"

Agnes looked grossed out, but also a little annoyed, as if Cordelia and Benji had been keeping a secret from her.

"Why didn't you tell me?" she asked.

"I'm not sure," Cordelia said, glancing at Benji. "It seemed like one of those things you don't mention. Like when someone has spinach between their teeth."

"It's not like that at all," Agnes muttered.

There was an awkward silence.

"The teachers said this happened before," Cordelia said, trying to change the topic. "What do you make of that?"

"Could have been the same guy," Benji said. "This poltergeist. It's not like he's getting any older."

"But *why*?"

"He's a ghost," Benji said. "He scares people. It's what he does."

"I don't buy that. There has to be a reason."

"Have you ever heard of a snakehead fish?" Agnes asked.

Cordelia and Benji exchanged a baffled look.

"They're fascinating," Agnes said. "Most people think they're scary, since they have these big yellow eyes and razor-sharp teeth—kind of like piranha, only snakeheads can grow up to four feet long. The *really* cool thing is that they can actually survive on land for a little while. This way when they run out of food in one body of water, they can slither across the grass to their next slaughtering ground."

"So killer fish that can walk," Cordelia said. "Thanks for the nightmares."

"Snakehead fish are indigenous to Asia and Africa," Agnes continued. "But about fifteen years ago, some idiot dumped a few northern snakeheads into a pond in Maryland, and now there are over twenty thousand of them up and down the Potomac River, eating everything in sight and making a mess of the entire ecosystem. It's not really their fault, though. The snakeheads were never supposed to be there in the first place."

"Like the ghosts were never supposed to be in Shadow School?" Cordelia asked, trying to figure out where Agnes was going with this. "They're the snakeheads?"

"No," Agnes said. "We are."

Cordelia shifted in her seat, trying to knead some sense out of Agnes's words. *Why is she comparing us to a hungry predator? All we've been trying to do is help.*

"I don't get it," she said.

"As far as I can tell, Shadow School was humming along just fine before us," Agnes said. "Ghosts were trapped in the school. They faded away. New ghosts replaced them. I don't pretend to understand what it means, but there was definitely a certain order to things—until we came along and started sending ghosts into the Bright. It was foolish of us to think there wouldn't be consequences. There has to be a reason why so many ghosts are trapped inside Shadow School. What if someone—like this poltergeist—wants it that way? And we're screwing it up?"

"Then why wouldn't he just stop us?" Benji asked.

"He might not know that we're the ones causing all the trouble," said Agnes. "Only that someone is messing with the way things are supposed to work. Maybe what happened today was a general warning. 'I know what you're doing. Now cut it out or else.' Could be that ten years ago, someone was freeing ghosts, exactly like us."

"You think it could have been the man who was killed?" Cordelia asked. "David Fisher?"

"Makes sense," Agnes said. "There's no reason to think that only kids can see ghosts. What if he was freeing them and didn't stop, so something made him disappear?"

Cordelia felt a chill run through her entire body. She had grown comfortable being around the ghosts. They were still scary, but as long as she was cautious, she believed she was safe.

If Agnes was right, it changed everything.

"Come on, guys," Benji said. "Ghosts are one thing. But the idea that we've made some telekinetic ghost angry? That seems a little far-fetched."

"More far-fetched than sending spirits to their own personal hereafter with baseball caps and eyeglasses?" Cordelia asked. "*Everything* about Shadow School is far-fetched! We have to at least consider the possibility that Agnes is right."

"Thank you," Agnes said, beaming with pride. "Obviously, the most logical plan from this point onward is to hold off on freeing any other ghosts until we have a better understanding of what we're—"

"Whoa!" Cordelia exclaimed, so loud that Agnes jumped in surprise. "We can't just stop. Those ghosts need us."

"I'm not saying we should stop forever," Agnes muttered, her previous confidence shattered. "But it might be a good idea to take some time off until we figure out what's going on here."

"And how many ghosts will vanish in the meantime?" Cordelia asked. "How many will we lose while we're sitting around doing nothing?"

"Not nothing," Agnes said. "Research. That's an important part of any scientific study."

"This isn't a scientific study, which you—" Cordelia swallowed the second part of her sentence: *which you would know if you could actually see them.* Agnes was sensitive about her inability to see the ghosts, viewing it as some kind of failure on her part. Criticizing her for it would be unfair and cruel.

"What do you think?" Cordelia asked, looking for an ally in Benji. "I mean, if this threat is so 'far-fetched,' like you said, then there's no reason to stop. Right?"

"Sorry," he said. "But I'm with Agnes on this one. We kind of jumped headfirst into this whole thing. It might be a good idea to take a step back and make sure we're not doing anything stupid."

"But the ghosts—"

"Are dead," Benji said. "We're not. I'd like to keep it that way."

"Well, I think we should keep helping them," Cordelia said, feeling her face grow warm as she tried to keep her temper in check. "But it's a group decision, so . . . whatever." She sighed and gave Agnes a begrudging smile. "I do agree that a little research is a good idea. It's time we figured out why all these ghosts are haunting Shadow School in the first place. And I know exactly where to start."

12

Archimancy

It was the day before holiday break, and no one, including the teachers, was taking school seriously. By mid-afternoon, Cordelia had completed two word searches, snipped out a blizzard's worth of snowflakes, played several "educational" games on the Chromebook, and helped Ms. Patel scrub down the beakers and graduated cylinders. Even Mrs. Machen was in a festive mood, giving them a packet full of fun puzzles instead of the usual worksheets. Benji called it a Christmas miracle.

At last they reached gym, the final block of the day. Cordelia and her friends had decided that this would be the best time to put their plan into action, so as soon as they arrived, she handed Mr. Bruce a small bag of chocolates tied with red and green ribbons.

"Happy holidays!" she exclaimed with her biggest smile. "I hope you like chocolate!"

"Thank you, Cordelia," Mr. Bruce said, looking surprised and a little touched. "I love chocolate." He patted his stomach over his Manchester United jersey. "Maybe a little too much."

"Oh no!" Cordelia exclaimed, as though she had just remembered something.

"What is it?"

"I got chocolate for Mr. Derleth too, but I forgot to give it to him! Is it okay if I run it over now?"

Mr. Bruce didn't normally allow his students to leave class, but either the holiday season or the unexpected gift had put him in a more lenient frame of mind.

"Sure thing; just make it quick."

After giving Agnes and Benji the thumbs-up sign to let them know that the first part of their plan had been a success, Cordelia grabbed a second bag of chocolates and quickly made her way to Mr. Derleth's room. Cordelia had peeked at the schedule hanging behind his desk and knew that he didn't have a class this period. If all went well, he would be alone in his room, either grading papers or preparing lessons. Cordelia wished Agnes and Benji were coming as well, but they had decided it would be better if only one of them spoke to Mr. Derleth. He had a fragile quality to him, like a wounded animal, and they didn't want to scare him off.

When Cordelia got there, the door was open. She knocked on it and peeked inside the room. Mr. Derleth was sitting at his desk holding a pair of small tongs in his hand. In front of him was a blue photo album, its binding cracked with age.

"Hey, Mr. Derleth," Cordelia said. "I brought you some chocolates!"

"You didn't have to do that, Cordelia," Mr. Derleth said. "But thank you. Come in."

Cordelia placed the bag of chocolates on the desk. The corners of Mr. Derleth's mouth twitched the slightest bit. It was the closest he ever came to a smile.

"What's this?" Cordelia asked, looking down at the photo album.

"A silly obsession of mine," Mr. Derleth said. "Philately. Stamp collecting. I started this collection when I was your age, and I guess I never really stopped." He slid the tongs, which were flat at the ends, into a small box on his desk and retrieved a stamp of a swallowtail butterfly worth thirteen cents. After a quick inspection, Mr. Derleth carefully added the stamp to a page that already had two neat rows of butterfly stamps.

"Cool," Cordelia said. The fact that he enjoyed

collecting stamps was the first personal thing that she had ever learned about Mr. Derleth. He didn't tell the class stories about his life like other teachers did. She didn't even know if he was married or had any children.

"There was actually something I wanted to ask you," Cordelia said. "Do you have a sec?"

Mr. Derleth placed the tongs on his desk and closed the album, giving her his full attention.

"Shoot," he said.

"The first day of school, you mentioned that Shadow School had an interesting history," Cordelia said. "I know that Elijah Shadow designed the building and then died in a fire, but I was hoping to learn more. There's nothing online, and the librarian at the public library could only find one brief mention in an architecture textbook."

"The Shadow family is secretive, to say the least," Mr. Derleth said. "I had to really do some digging. Old letters, public documents, journals. Things like that. What is it you want to know?"

"Everything," Cordelia said.

Mr. Derleth scratched his beard, mulling this over. He seemed perplexed by Cordelia's interest, but intrigued as well.

"Elijah Shadow was a genius," he said. "The son of two former slaves, without any formal schooling—and yet he still managed to become a renowned architect at a very young age. This was the late 1800s, mind you, not so long after the Civil War. For a black man to be designing mansions for wealthy white people—you understand how impressive that was?"

"I don't think I can," Cordelia said.

"No," Mr. Derleth said. "Me either. But I imagine he had to be twenty times better than any other architect just to stay in business. It helped that he married his childhood sweetheart, Hallie Washington. She was his rock in hard times. The 1800s became the 1900s, and they had a baby girl, Wilma. Life was good."

Mr. Derleth's features grew grim. Cordelia could tell that the story was about to take a dark turn.

"The baby died, didn't she?" Cordelia asked in a quiet voice.

"No," Mr. Derleth said. "I'm happy to report that Wilma lived to a ripe old age. Married a haberdasher, had a boatload of children. But Elijah's wife, Hallie—that was a different story. She died of tuberculosis when their daughter was barely out of the cradle, and a part of Elijah died with her. He stopped working and refused to leave the house. Then one night he woke up and saw his wife's spirit standing over their daughter, watching her sleep. She vanished the moment he stepped into the room. Elijah's friends tried to convince him that his grief was making him imagine things, but he wouldn't listen. He became obsessed with ghosts."

Cordelia leaned forward, eager to learn more, but Mr. Derleth stopped talking and stroked his beard.

"I'm not sure if I should tell you this next part," he said. "I don't want to give you nightmares."

"Don't worry. I don't scare easily."

He searched her face for a moment.

"No," he said. "I don't imagine you do." Mr. Derleth looked like he was about to ask her something and then changed her mind. "Elijah Shadow became convinced that his wife was still out there, if he could only learn how to speak to her. At first, he tried all the traditional things—seances, spiritualists, Ouija boards—but he quickly determined that this was all nonsense and decided to conduct his own research. He sold his house and all his worldly possessions, and he and little Wilma toured the country, investigating hundreds of so-called haunted houses. Most times there was nothing to it. But on those rare occasions when Shadow found irrefutable evidence that a haunting was truly taking place, he ignored the ghost completely and studied the house."

Mr. Derleth's eyes sparked to life as he passed along the things he had learned. His posture bespoke a deep and abiding sadness, but the man clearly enjoyed teaching.

"First Shadow examined the house's blueprints and filled notebook after notebook with meticulous figures. Then he made lists of what materials were used and where, the number of panes in each window, the height of the chimney, which side faced the sun in the morning, the slope of the roof . . . you get the point. Shadow did this with every house he deemed legitimately haunted. And over many years, he came to believe that certain hauntings had nothing to do with restless spirits, but rather *the way the house had been built.*"

Cordelia felt a tingling in her scalp, like finally recognizing a landmark after being totally lost for hours. *Yes*, she thought. *This is it! This is what I need to know!*

"According to Elijah Shadow," Mr. Derleth said, "there was a certain confluence of architectural elements—the precise right building materials constructed in the precise right way—that created a sort of trap for ghosts. It only happened by pure accident once in a blue moon. Those are your traditional haunted houses. But Shadow believed that if he studied these houses and tracked the similarities between them, he could use this knowledge to build a haunted house *on purpose.* He called this process archimancy."

"That's how he built Shadow School, isn't it?" Cordelia asked. "He wanted it to be haunted!" The idea, and all its implications, stampeded through her brain. *That's why there are so many ghosts! The building itself is designed to keep them here!*

"Correct," Mr. Derleth said, giving her a curious look as though surprised by how quickly she had made the connection. "And not just any haunted house, mind you. Shadow believed he could use archimancy to amplify a building's 'ghost-trapping' qualities. In short, he wanted Shadow School to be the most haunted house in the world." The teacher folded his hands together and regarded her carefully. "I've answered your question, Cordelia. Now it's my turn. You don't seem particularly shocked by any of this. Surprised—yes. But not shocked. So I have to ask: Have you seen any ghosts?"

Mr. Derleth had caught her off guard with his question, and Cordelia hesitated before answering.

"No," she said. "Of course not. I mean, ghosts aren't real."

"Are you sure?" Mr. Derleth asked. "You can trust me if you've seen something unusual, Cordelia. Maybe we can help each other."

Cordelia considered telling him the truth. *He knows so much about the school,* she thought. *He might be able to help us.* It wasn't a decision she could make without talking to Agnes and Benji first, however, and while

129

she liked Mr. Derleth, there was something about him she didn't trust. He seemed far too anxious to find out what she knew.

"The scariest thing I've seen at Shadow School is the geometry test I took last week," Cordelia said. "There's no such thing as ghosts. Elijah Shadow was clearly bonkers."

"Perhaps," Mr. Derleth said. "Except—there is one thing. I wouldn't necessarily call it proof, but . . . by the end of his haunted house tour, Shadow didn't have a penny to his name." He raised his arm to encompass all of Shadow School. "Which raises the question: How did he manage to build such a lavish and expensive home? I didn't learn much from the financial records of the Shadow family, which are conveniently missing entire years. It took me a long time to find the answer."

He reached into the side drawer of his desk and produced a manila folder overflowing with papers.

"Arend Meulenbelt was a young man from a prominent Dutch family," Mr. Derleth said, riffling through the papers in the folder. "While visiting America for the first time, he heard whispers of a secret show held by a Mr. Elijah Shadow, with a ridiculously high admission price that only the upper class could afford. Supposedly, the American would display several ghosts that he had captured, with a clever catch: only the truly gifted would be able to see them. Well, of course everyone claimed they could see the ghosts whether they really could or not—they'd obviously never read 'The Emperor's New Clothes.' But Arend swore that he really did see spirits. He even drew them."

Mr. Derleth pulled out a yellowed piece of paper that had been torn apart at one time and pieced back together again. It was a sketch drawn with pencils and a hint of charcoal: a row of boxes with circular viewing windows and pale faces trapped behind the glass. There was a date at the bottom—1912—and a scribbled signature.

This must have been how Elijah started, Cordelia thought. *Trapping ghosts in boxes before he learned how to trap them in an entire house.*

"He's a good artist," Cordelia said, trying to keep her face as impassive as possible. "With a great imagination."

"I suppose so," Mr. Derleth said.

He searched her eyes for a moment, and then slid the sketch back into the folder.

"Thanks for telling me all this," Cordelia said, rising to leave. "It was really interesting."

"Thanks for listening, Cordelia," Mr. Derleth said, turning his attention back to his stamp collection. The bags beneath his eyes seemed more swollen than usual.

Cordelia remembered her mom mentioning that for some people, the holiday season could be the saddest time of the year.

"Have a good break, Mr. Derleth," Cordelia said.

"You too. And thanks again for the chocolate."

He placed another stamp in the album. His hand trembled.

Notes

The hallways were quiet as the school settled down for a long winter's nap. Cordelia, who could now navigate its labyrinthine corridors as well as anyone, hustled toward her locker. She had a good ten minutes before the bus came, but she was excited to get to her phone and let Agnes and Benji know what she had learned.

Inside the slots of her locker door was a yellow sticky note. She unfolded it and read:

New one in boiler room. Check it out before you leave.

—B

Benji had never left her a note before, so Cordelia was curious what was so special about this particular ghost. *I can take a quick peek and still make the bus*, she thought, grabbing her backpack. She ran downstairs and made it to the boiler room in record time. After waiting for a group of girls singing Christmas carols to pass, Cordelia opened the door and descended a short flight of steps to a pitted concrete floor stained with oil. The only light came from a work lamp in the corner. Metal shelves sagged beneath cardboard boxes and rusty machinery, while an ancient furnace hissed its complaints.

Cordelia squinted her eyes, looking for the ghost. She couldn't see anything in the immediate vicinity, but on the other side of the room lay a patch of darkness beyond the limited scope of the work lamp. *Maybe there?* she thought.

The door clicked shut behind her.

Cordelia scaled the steps in two giant leaps and tried to turn the knob. It was locked. "Hey!" she exclaimed, slamming her fists against the solid metallic surface. "Let me out!" She caught a flash of movement beneath the door and bent down to take a look. Someone was standing there, just a few inches away.

"Hello?" Cordelia asked quietly. She was a little

134

scared now. *Why aren't they opening the door?* "Is some-one there?"

A single piece of paper slid through the gap and fluttered down the steps. Cordelia picked it up and brought it over to the work light. It was a Post-it note just like the one she had found in her locker. Three words had been written with a black Sharpie:

STOP HELPING THEM

The shadow beneath the door vanished. Cordelia screamed some more, hoping that someone else might hear her. No one came.

Benji didn't write that note, she thought. *It was the person who locked me in here. This was a trap. Someone knows what we're doing and wants us to stop it.* Cordelia couldn't imagine the kind of person who would lock a child in a boiler room. *Is it someone I know? A teacher? And how did they know that we've been helping ghosts?*

Cordelia would worry about that later—*after* she got out of there.

"My phone!" she remembered, giddy with relief. She would just call the main office, and if that didn't work, she'd call her parents. Cordelia slung off her bookbag and reached inside the pocket where she normally kept her phone. It wasn't there. She checked the other pockets, then finally emptied the contents of her bag onto the floor.

No phone.

The same person who locked me in here must have stolen my phone, she thought. This didn't narrow down the possibilities as far as their identity went; Cordelia's lock had been issued by the school, and any employee had access to the combination. It did, however, send the first trickles of true fear down her spine. *If they took my phone, they really thought this through. They don't want me getting out of here at all.*

Cordelia took a few deep breaths, forcing herself to remain calm. She carefully examined the room, struggling to figure out her next step. *Maybe there's another door. Or a duct I can crawl through.* She waved the work light from place to place.

A small figure watched her from beneath a workbench.

Cordelia screamed in surprise. After the initial shock, however, she quickly recognized the familiar blue eyes and glasses, the pajamas lined with trains.

"Hey," Cordelia said, giving the boy a bright smile.

He stepped into the light, hands folded shyly together. Cordelia realized that her horrified reaction had probably frightened him a lot more than he frightened her.

He wore the downtrodden expression of a child about to get scolded.

"I'm sorry I screamed," Cordelia said in a gentle voice. "You surprised me. That's all. I'm really glad to see you."

The boy breathed a sigh of relief.

"How did you get out of the gym?" Cordelia asked. "I thought you were trapped there."

The boy pointed at Cordelia.

"Me?" she asked.

He nodded.

"That doesn't make any sense," Cordelia said. "I had nothing to do with it."

The boy shook his head and pointed at her again.

"Okay," Cordelia said. "One thing at a time. You're here, and that's all that matters." She pointed to the top of the stairs. "I need to get through that door. Can you help?"

The boy broke into a huge grin and gave her a little bow: *At your service*. Cordelia noticed that he was missing a tooth. She suspected that it would be missing forever. The idea filled her with sorrow.

He seems so alive, she thought.

The boy ran up the stairs—his footsteps making no sound—and passed through the red door as though it wasn't there at all. A few moments later, he poked his head back into the room and waved her forward: *Come on! What are you waiting for?*

"I'm not a ghost," Cordelia said. "I can't walk through solid doors."

The boy smacked his head—*Duh!*

"No worries," Cordelia said. "Any other ideas?"

The boy held up his index finger: *I'll be right back.*

"I'll be here," Cordelia said with a wry grin.

The boy was gone longer this time. Cordelia paced the floor. She wished the boy could simply open the door, but of course that was impossible. The only thing ghosts could physically touch were their Brightkeys. A black thought hatched, further fueling her panic: *It's the day before holiday break. Once everyone goes home, this building is going to be empty for a long, long time.* If Cordelia had been thinking rationally, she would have realized that her parents would demand a search of Shadow School when she didn't come home on the bus. But Cordelia wasn't thinking rationally. Right now, all she could focus on was what it would be like to try to survive ten days without food or water in this dark, subterranean room.

A few minutes later, just as Cordelia was beginning to wonder if shutting off the furnace might make someone come investigate, the boy leaped out of the wall to her right. Cordelia's heart did a triple somersault in her chest.

"You have to knock or something before you do that," she said.

The boy ignored her and pointed to the wall, his face glowing with excitement. He had never looked more alive.

"Seriously?" Cordelia asked. "This is your way out?" She knew the boy meant well, but she was scared out of her wits and running out of patience. "I can't pass through a wall any easier than I can pass through a door."

The boy shook his head and jabbed his finger forward. Cordelia realized that he wasn't pointing at the entire wall but a specific cinder block. Curious, she ran her hand over the spot. It felt different. Smoother. Cordelia dug her nail inside a long scratch and heard something snap, like the clasp of a battery case.

A lid fell open.

The cinder block was hollow. It contained a flashlight and a wooden lever that protruded from the interior of the wall.

"Hmm," Cordelia said, taking the flashlight. "Guess there's only one thing you can do with a lever."

She pulled it.

Gears instantly clicked into action, the wall parting as individual cinder blocks slid back and then re-formed into a tiny set of stairs. Everything ran as smooth as clockwork. Cordelia hadn't decided if Elijah Shadow was a good man or a bad man, but one thing was certain: he was a brilliant architect.

Plus there's an honest-to-god secret passageway in my school, she thought. *And there's no reality where that's not super cool.*

Cordelia peeked through the opening. It smelled musty and old. She heard the pitter-patter of mice disturbed by the tremors she had sent through their world.

"Lead the way," Cordelia told the boy.

He smiled and ascended the stairs. Cordelia clicked on the flashlight and crossed the threshold. She must have tripped some kind of mechanism in the process, because the wall sealed shut behind them.

Behind the Walls

At the top of the stairs, the narrow passageway grew just wide enough for Cordelia and the boy to walk side by side. It was colder here, a welcome reprieve from the heat of the boiler room. The wooden floor creaked beneath Cordelia's sneakers but made no sound at all beneath the boy's bare feet.

Although she was anxious to get somewhere safe, Cordelia's curiosity refused to be subdued. She found herself shining the flashlight in all directions, eager to explore this hidden world.

"This is weird," Cordelia said, "even by Shadow School standards."

Cordelia's parents were obsessed with HGTV,

especially the kind of show where they took a bad house, tore it apart, and remade it into something beautiful. In Cordelia's opinion, once you saw one episode, you had seen them all. There was usually popcorn, however, and she liked sitting between her parents and hearing the jokes that passed between them.

Consequently, she had a general idea of what a house was supposed to look like behind its walls. Long wooden studs nailed together into rows of precisely measured frames. Pink insulation like the bedding for some giant guinea pig. A network of metal pipes.

Shadow School was different.

The bays between each wooden frame weren't open, like in a regular house. Instead, they were covered by elaborate, symmetrical patterns that resembled webs, if spiders spun wood and wire instead of silk. No two were exactly alike. Some webs were perfect tessellations. Others displayed elaborate designs that seemed random at first, but upon further investigation hinted at a mysterious order. Triangles and pyramids were the dominant shapes.

The boy tapped his foot against the floor, eager to move on.

"Hold your horses," Cordelia said, one of her mother's favorite expressions. She shone her light on one of the webs. "Look at all these triangles. It's just like the portals when ghosts enter their Brights."

Cordelia noticed a copper wire, as thin as fishing line, running from the web to a slightly thicker copper wire that hung from the ceiling. Investigating further, Cordelia saw that all the webs were likewise connected to this main wire, which ran parallel to the floor in either direction.

"What's this?" Cordelia asked. She hesitantly reached out and touched the wire with the tip of her index finger. A humming jolt passed through her body, like some kind of low-voltage electricity. Cordelia jerked her hand back in surprise.

When she turned around, the boy was facing her with arms crossed and a displeased expression on his face, as though she were a disobedient child.

"What?" Cordelia asked. "I was *curious.*"

The boy jabbed his finger forward: *Hurry up!* He looked around with genuine fear in his eyes, as though he was afraid that they might get caught if they stayed too long. Cordelia didn't know what, exactly, the boy was afraid of, but she didn't like the idea of something scary enough to frighten a ghost.

She walked faster.

"I'll have to come back here with Agnes and Benji," she said. "They'll want to see this. Well, Agnes at least."

Cordelia wasn't sure if she was talking to the boy

or herself. Mostly she wanted to fill the silence, which was almost as frightening as the darkness that pressed against them on all sides.

"Who do you think left this?" she asked, turning the flashlight in her hand. It looked fairly new. "Whoever it is, they definitely know about this passageway. I wonder what else they know about. Do you think they're the ones who trapped me in the boiler room?"

The boy shrugged.

They reached their first corner. A black pyramid stood in their path. It was solid on two sides, but open in the front and back, leaving enough room for an average-sized adult to pass through it. The apex of this pyramid was connected to the copper wire that ran along the ceiling, which made a sharp right angle before continuing into the dark.

The boy stepped through the pyramid. Cordelia took a deep breath and followed him, feeling a prickling along her skin similar to when she had touched the copper wire.

Suddenly the idea that Elijah Shadow could imprison the dead through some kind of magical architecture didn't seem so crazy at all.

A few minutes later she found another lever to pull. After a parting of cinder blocks similar to the one that had happened in the boiler room, Cordelia stepped into a supply closet. Dusty textbooks that hadn't been read in years lined the shelves.

The wall closed up behind her.

"We're back!" Cordelia exclaimed, smiling down at the boy. She opened her arms to give him a hug and quickly lowered them, realizing that she couldn't. The boy's smile faltered.

"I couldn't have gotten out of there without you," Cordelia said. "You're my hero. No matter what."

She exited the closet and found herself in the third-floor hallway. The lights were off. Night had fallen, and snow swirled against the windows. Cordelia headed for the stairs, thinking that she should check her locker first to see if her phone had simply fallen out of her bag. If it wasn't there, she'd find a phone in the main office or one of the classrooms. And then, when she got home, she was going to have a long conversation with Benji and Agnes. *There's so much to tell them*, she thought, floored by how much she had learned in the past few hours. *Archimancy. The boy breaking ghost rules. Secret passageway. Pyramids.*

Cordelia heard a rolling, rattling noise from around the bend, like an approaching cart. She started to call out for help, thinking it was one of the custodians working late, but the moment she opened her mouth, a terrible coldness numbed her fingers. Cordelia snapped

145

her hand away and glared down at the boy, who had resorted to touching her in order to get her attention.

He held a single finger to his lips: *Shhh.*

"Who is that?" Cordelia whispered, turning off the flashlight. "Who's coming?"

The boy took a step into the shadows and gestured for Cordelia to join him. The moment she did, a man crossed the intersection at the end of the hall. He was heavyset and wearing navy blue coveralls. Cordelia didn't remember seeing him around Shadow School, but he certainly looked like he worked there; he was pushing a cart holding a black trash can and an assortment of cleaning supplies. For a moment, she was certain that the boy had been worried for no reason at all.

Then the custodian passed beneath a window and the moonlight shone through his transparent body.

He's a ghost, she thought.

The spirit continued out of sight. A few moments later, the rattling sound of the cleaning cart came to a sudden halt.

"I need to see what he's up to," Cordelia told the boy, who frantically shook his head in response. "I'll be fine. You stay here."

She crept out of the shadows and poked her head around the corner. The ghost was about three classrooms away, getting something from his cart. His back was facing her. Cordelia used this opportunity to dash across the hall and duck into an alcove for a better vantage point. Though the hallway was dark, light shone through the open door of a nearby classroom, allowing her to see the ghost clearly. He was in his fifties, with thinning hair and a patch on his coveralls that said *Lenny*. As she watched, Lenny set up two A-frame signs about twenty feet from the left and right of the cart, moving with the bone-weary, slumped-shoulder gait of a working man at the end of a long shift. The signs were the same size and shape as the kind that read "Caution: Wet Floor," except these were black with no words at all.

Cordelia caught a flash of movement and realized there was a second figure doing its best to melt into the shadows: the ghost of a young man with one of those hipster beards that made him look like a barista in a trendy café. She passed him every day on the way to science. He spent his days staring out the window, like many spirits, and making a spinning motion with his finger. They hadn't figured out why yet.

The ghost wasn't spinning his finger now, however. He looked terrified.

What's going on here? Cordelia wondered.

Lenny rapped on the garbage can with his knuckles,

producing a deafening noise like a metallic thunder-clap. Cordelia clapped her hands to her ears and turned away. When she looked back, two new figures had appeared just beyond the fringe of light. Lenny nodded toward the hipster ghost doing its best to hide, and the first figure stepped out of the darkness. He was a young man with slicked-back hair wearing gray work clothes from an older generation, the pants sitting high on his waist, with a button-down shirt tucked in tight.

He began to whistle.

It was a lullaby, each note in impossible harmony with itself, as though there were a chorus of whistlers instead of just one. Cordelia felt her limbs grow sluggish and saw that the boy, who had at some point rejoined her, could barely stay awake. His eyes fluttered, and he tottered uneasily from side to side before falling through the wall. The hipster ghost had also fallen asleep, collapsing to the hallway floor.

The whistling ghost passed a hallway mirror and pulled a comb out of his back pocket. He ran it through his hair while admiring his reflection.

The second figure stepped out of the darkness.

It was the same man Cordelia had seen in the lunchroom. He wasn't wearing his tinted goggles today. Cordelia wished he was. There was no emotion in his green eyes, no capacity for kindness. He marched forward with precise, measured strides and removed a clipboard from the side of the cart. She had no idea how long it had been since he was alive, but she suspected it was during a time where people rode horses to get where they needed to go.

I should have listened to the boy and gotten out of here while I could, she thought, pressing her back against the wall in order to remain completely out of sight. The first two ghosts were scary enough, but the ghost with the green eyes—the *poltergeist*, she reminded herself—was something different altogether. Cordelia didn't want to think about what might happen if he found her spying on them.

Still, she had to know what the three of them were doing. And so, after gathering her courage, Cordelia peeked around the corner.

The green-eyed ghost reached into the cart and withdrew a long, wrought-iron tool that looked as though it had been forged by a blacksmith. It had a large pincer on one end, black and jagged like the claw of a prehistoric crustacean; in general, it reminded Cordelia of the grabber tools that custodians used to pick up trash. While the whistler continued his soporific tune, the green-eyed ghost dug the pincer into the back of the hipster and pressed a trigger at the opposite end. The edges of the pincer closed. The green-eyed ghost pulled backward, and the hipster seemed to leap out of himself, though the version gripped by the pincer quickly deflated and hung like a suit of clothes. Lenny opened the lid of the garbage can, and the green-eyed ghost dumped what he had stolen from the hipster.

Whistler stopped whistling. The hipster ghost sat up. He had been solid before, but now Cordelia could see right through him.

That's why the ghosts fade away over time, she thought, pressing her back against the wall so she didn't have to look anymore. *These monsters come in the night and snatch a part of them!* She heard the lid of the garbage can close and the cart begin to rumble away. Cordelia was about to risk a peek when the boy popped out of the wall, stretching his arms as though he had just woken from a nap. His sudden appearance was more than her frazzled nerves could take, and a tiny shriek escaped her lips.

The cart stopped moving.

Cordelia looked down the hall and saw the green-eyed ghost heading in their direction. She held her breath and remained perfectly still, hoping the darkness would be deep enough to cloak her. *Ghosts can't see the living that well*, she thought, her heart fluttering in her chest. *Just don't move.* As far as she could tell, her plan was working. The ghost squinted in her general direction, but he couldn't seem to pin down her location. Unfortunately, he had no problem seeing the boy. The green-eyed ghost seemed both angered and bewildered by his presence, as though aware that the boy belonged behind the bleachers and not in this part of the school.

"Get out of here," Cordelia whispered. "Run!"

The boy was too overcome by fear to move, and there was no way for Cordelia to grab his hand and get him started. With no idea what else to do, she reared back and threw the flashlight as hard as she could. It passed through the ghost's body, slid along the floor, and made a clanking noise against the cart.

The ghost snatcher swiveled his head in her direction. This time he saw her for sure.

Cordelia turned to run, but before she had gone four steps, the hallway lights came to life, and three living, breathing, beautiful adults were running toward her: Mr. Ward, his keys in his hand, Mr. Derleth, and her mother. The ghost snatchers and their cart were nowhere to be seen.

"Cordelia!" Mrs. Liu exclaimed.

Cordelia ran into her mother's arms. She smelled of sandalwood soap and safety.

"I was *so worried*!" she exclaimed. "What *happened*?"

Cordelia froze, unsure what to say, but luckily Mrs. Liu kept talking. "Wait. I have to call your dad and tell him everything is okay. He's waiting at home in case you came back, worried sick. And then you need to tell us *everything.*"

By the time Mrs. Liu got off the phone, Cordelia had formulated her story.

"I was heading to the bus when I dropped my phone," Cordelia said. "Some eighth grader in a hurry accidentally kicked it down the stairs of the boiler room. When I went to get it, the door shut behind me and I got locked in."

It was a pretty lame story, but Cordelia knew she couldn't tell the truth. If her parents knew how dangerous Shadow School really was, they would never let her stay. *And who will keep the boy safe then?* she thought, giving the ghost a secretive wave. He waved in return and vanished through the wall.

"Well, I'm just glad you're okay, sweetie," Mrs. Liu said. "That's all that—"

"How'd you get out?" Mr. Derleth asked.

"Hmm?" said Cordelia.

"You said the door locked behind you. So how'd you get out?"

Mr. Derleth met her eyes. *He knows I'm lying,*

152

Cordelia thought. *Is that because he's the one who locked me in the boiler room to begin with?*

"It turned out the door was just stuck, not locked," Cordelia said. "All I needed to do was shove it hard enough."

"Ahh," said Mr. Derleth. "How fortunate."

"Well, thank you for helping me look, Mr. Derleth," Mrs. Liu said, shaking his hand. "It's lucky you were still in the building." She turned to Mr. Ward. "And thank you so much as well. I'm sorry if I ruined your night."

"You can show yourselves out," Mr. Ward said. "I'm going to stick behind and lock up." He gave Mr. Derleth a suspicious look. "And if you don't mind, I think it's time for you to head out as well. Dr. Roqueni expects students *and* teachers out of here by nightfall."

"Why is that again?" Mr. Derleth asked.

"Because that's when I turn off the heat and electricity," Mr. Ward said, taking a threatening step in Mr. Derleth's direction. "It's . . . what do you call it? A green initiative. Reducing our carbon footprint. Dr. Roqueni is all about helping the environment."

"Inspiring," Mr. Derleth said. "Well, I was just about to leave anyway. Pleasure to meet you, Mrs. Liu. Good night, Cordelia. I'm glad to see you safe and sound."

Mrs. Liu placed a protective arm around Cordelia's shoulders and guided her away. Just before they turned the corner, Cordelia glanced back at Mr. Ward. He was staring down at the broken flashlight on the floor, as though wondering how it had gotten there.

15

An Unexpected Trip

It was Christmas morning. While her parents drank coffee on the sofa, Cordelia opened her presents. The last one was a long, thin box with an elaborate bow. Inside, nestled between several layers of red tissue paper, was a plane ticket to California.

Cordelia looked up at her parents, stunned.

"Is this real?" she asked.

"Be pretty mean if it wasn't," Mrs. Liu said, taking her husband's hand. "We're spending the rest of December there! Your friends can't wait to see you!"

Cordelia squealed and hugged them.

"Thank you, thank you, thank you! This is the best present *ever*!"

And so, two days later, Cordelia found herself sitting on the beach with her old friends, staring out at the Pacific Ocean. They asked Cordelia what her school was like and whether her teachers were nice. Cordelia told them what answers she could. They laughed a lot and built a bad sand castle and swore that this was going to be the greatest school break of all time.

By the end of the first day, Cordelia was bored out of her mind.

Her friends hadn't changed. Mabel was still sweet and bubbly. Ava was still a good listener. They had been nice girls when Cordelia lived here, and they were nice girls now.

The problem was her.

Things that used to seem important now felt like a total waste of time. Cordelia couldn't feign interest in the cute boy that Ava liked or Mabel's latest swim medal when the ghosts of Shadow School were in such terrible danger. Her mind kept wandering to the boy. She pictured him alone in that dark school, the ghost snatchers stalking him through the corridors. Cordelia was the only one who could help him, but she was trapped three thousand miles away, whiling away the hours watching bad movies or strolling through the mall.

She grew sullen and snappy. By the third day, Mabel

and Ava said they had plans and couldn't hang out. Cordelia didn't blame them.

The Lius flew home a day earlier than planned.

On the night of New Year's Eve, Benji and Agnes came to Cordelia's house to watch the ball drop on TV. Cordelia made sure they had better snacks this time: pretzels, nachos, salsa, pepperoni and cheese, and three types of soda. Agnes even added some homemade peanut brittle. Cordelia had never seen Benji look so happy.

They settled into the couches and left the TV volume on low. The basement was colder than the rest of the house. Cordelia shared a blanket with Agnes.

"I have so many questions," Agnes said after Mr. and Mrs. Liu had gone upstairs. "I don't even know where to begin." Cordelia had already texted them about her frightening experience with the ghost snatchers, but this was the first time they had talked about it in person.

"I'll start," Benji said. "Why are there *pyramids* behind the walls of our school?"

"And when do we get to see them?" Agnes added eagerly.

"I thought about the secret passageway a lot while I was in California," Cordelia said. "And I think the whole weird setup has to do with the thing Mr. Derleth was talking about. Archimancy. The pyramids and wires must be necessary for the school to attract ghosts—and keep them trapped inside."

"You really think that's the reason the school is haunted?" Benji asked. "Because of the way it's built?"

"It makes as much sense as anything else," Cordelia said.

"The only way we'll know for sure is if we investigate this passageway of yours," Agnes said. "Take photos. Gather samples."

"Soon. For now, I think we should concentrate on these guys."

Cordelia handed them a sketch of the ghost snatchers. She had used graphite pencils to draw the bodies and a bright-green pastel to emphasize the otherworldly nature of the poltergeist's eyes. It wasn't her best work, but judging from the way the color drained from Benji's face, it got the point across.

"I've never seen these ghosts before," Benji said.

"I think they only come out at night after everyone else has left," Cordelia said. "That's when they do their job."

"Ghosts have jobs?" Benji asked.

"Or something like it," Cordelia said. "There's even this clipboard with some kind of list, I guess, like they have a certain number of ghosts they have to . . ." She struggled to find the right word. "Collect? Except that's not right, because they don't take the whole ghost at once."

"What about 'peel'?" Agnes suggested. "It's kind of gross, but isn't that what they're doing? Peeling one layer after another until there's no more ghost left."

Cordelia shuddered. The word fit, but that didn't mean she had to like it.

"I thought the ghosts just faded away because that's what happened," Benji said. "Like getting old for dead people. But it's been these ghost snatchers the entire time."

"Which is why the ghosts vanish in three stages instead of gradually," Agnes said, thinking it through. "Three visits from the ghost snatchers. That's all they get. I wonder, though. Do you think this is how it works with ghosts all over the world, or is this just a Shadow School thing?"

"Why does it matter?" Cordelia asked. "They're evil, and we have to stop them."

"It might not be that simple."

"It really is," Cordelia said.

Agnes looked like she wanted to say more, but she held her tongue for the time being.

"Guess we know why the leader caused all that trouble in the lunchroom," Benji said. "He was warning us not to send any more ghosts to the Bright. Getting rid of them is his job. Could he have been the one who locked you in the boiler room?"

"No way," Cordelia said. "Ghosts don't leave notes and hide cell phones. That was a living, breathing person."

Benji buried his face in his hands.

"As if having ghosts who hate us wasn't enough," he muttered.

"Could it be a student?" Agnes asked.

"I doubt it," Cordelia said. "The boiler room doesn't lock on its own. You need the key."

"It's hard to believe a teacher would lock you up like that," Benji said.

Cordelia knew how he felt. The idea that a grown-up they knew and trusted meant them harm was almost as scary as the ghost snatchers.

"Would a teacher even have a key to the furnace room?" Agnes asked. "Maybe it was someone from the office. Or Mr. Ward. He has the keys to everything."

Benji shook his head.

"I know Mr. Ward looks a little scary," he said, "but he's a good guy. Last year he saw how Mason and some of the other boys were getting on my case at recess, so he let me hide in the back of the school and play soccer. He even shares these Greek pastries that his wife makes

160

sometimes. Does that sound like the kind of guy who would threaten an eleven-year-old girl?"

"I guess not," Cordelia said. "So who?"

They thought about this. On TV, a pop star performed her latest hit in front of the massive crowd in Times Square. She looked cold.

"Let's focus on what we know for sure," Agnes finally said. "Whoever gave you that note definitely knew what we've been up to with the ghosts. Did you guys tell anyone besides me?"

"No one," Cordelia said.

"Me either," said Benji.

"Then someone must have seen you send a ghost into the Bright," Agnes said. "Like I did the first time. Who could that be?"

Cordelia considered the question for a moment before answering.

"Mrs. Machen is always around after school, making her packets. She's given us a couple of suspicious looks."

"I think that's just her regular look," Benji said.

"And since I talk to the boy almost every day, I guess Mr. Bruce could have seen me at some point." Cordelia paused. "We shouldn't rule out Mr. Derleth, either. He knows an awful lot about the school, and I have this feeling that he's hiding something. Plus, he was in Shadow School that night. Kind of a strange coincidence."

"In conclusion," Benji said, "we have no idea who locked you in the boiler room or why they want us to stop freeing the ghosts. Is there anything we *do* know?"

"I know I'm tired," Cordelia said, yawning.

"It's almost midnight," Agnes said. She turned up the volume on the TV. "Try to stay up just a little while longer."

Benji blew a noisemaker in Cordelia's face.

"That's what's going to happen every time you close your eyes," he said. "Annoying, isn't it?"

"*You're* annoying," said Cordelia. She tried to grab the noisemaker from his hand, but Benji was too quick, so she smacked him with a pillow instead.

"That's better," Agnes said, smiling.

In the end, Cordelia managed to stay awake until midnight. The old year died. A new one was born.

16

The Search

On the morning they returned to school, Cordelia flew off the bus and ran straight to the gym. Much to her surprise, Mr. Bruce was already there.

"Good morning," Cordelia said, trying to hide her annoyance. The gym teacher, who was going retro with a Milwaukee Braves jersey today, usually hung out in the teachers' lounge until homeroom ended. "How was your break?"

"Short," Mr. Bruce said. "How about you?"

"Great," Cordelia said. The boy had stopped crying weeks ago, so there was no way to tell if he was there without actually looking. "I think I might have dropped something behind the bleachers. Okay if I check?"

"I took a peek this morning," Mr. Bruce said as he placed orange traffic cones around the gym. "Nothing back there but dust. You're buddies with Benji Núñez, right?"

"I guess."

"Spring soccer sign-ups are soon," he said. "Think you can mention it? I'd love to have him back on the team. It's a shame to let all that talent go to waste."

"I'll pass it along," Cordelia said. "The thing I dropped behind the bleachers—it's an earring. Super small. You might have missed it."

Mr. Bruce shrugged.

"Knock yourself out."

"Thanks," Cordelia said. She crossed the gym at a run, eager to see the boy's smiling face.

He wasn't there.

Cordelia checked the gym three more times that morning, with no luck. By lunch she was in a state of panic. She sat across the table from Benji and Agnes, ignoring her food completely. She felt too queasy to eat.

"We have to find him," she said.

"Why?" Benji asked. He was wearing a new hoodie that looked exactly like his other hoodies. "You said the kid could go anywhere he wants to now. How long was he trapped under those bleachers? If I was him, I'd never step foot inside that gym again!"

"You don't understand," Cordelia said. "Even if the boy was out and about, he would have gone back to the gym the moment he saw people in the school again. He'd know that's where I'd look for him." She felt tears coming on and squeezed her eyes shut. "Something's wrong."

Agnes leaned over and put her arm around her shoulder.

"I'll make you brownies tonight," she said. "With coconut."

"And I'll help you look after school," Benji said. "You in, Ag?"

"I promised my parents I'd do a board game marathon with them," she said. "I know it's kind of dorky, but—"

"Nah," Benji said. "It's nice."

"Besides," Agnes said, rolling a tater tot from one side of her tray to the other, "it's not like I can really help you look for him." Her expression grew worried. "What if the person who locked you in the boiler room sees you? Remember what the note said? 'Stop helping them.'"

"I don't care," Cordelia said.

"I think that's a warning not to send ghosts to the Bright," Benji said. "This is strictly search and rescue.

Should be fine."

"We haven't actually freed a ghost in a long time," Cordelia said. "I miss it. Do you think maybe we could—"

"It's riskier now than ever," Agnes said, keeping her voice to a whisper.

"You're right," Benji said. "But I liked helping the ghosts. For the first time in my life, I felt like I was doing something good. Not helping-my-mom-with-the-dishes good. The real deal."

"Me too," Cordelia said.

"It feels wrong just stopping because someone told us to. Like giving up. But I keep asking myself: What exactly have we gotten ourselves into? There's so much we don't understand. I'm scared that we're going to do something incredibly stupid and not realize it until it's too late."

"Let's find the boy first," Cordelia said, "and see what happens."

Auditions for the spring musical were being held after school that day, giving Cordelia a ready-made excuse to stay—though she had to promise to text her mom every half hour. Considering everything that she had put her through, Cordelia thought this was more than fair.

She met Benji at the lockers.

"Come on," Cordelia said, grabbing his arm and pulling him along. "We only have seven minutes to get to the copy machine!"

"Don't you want to search the classrooms?" Benji asked.

"No need. The boy's not going to hide in such an obvious spot."

"What about that secret passageway you found?"

"Possibly," Cordelia replied. "But let's try the attic first. I told the boy what happened to Elijah Shadow, and all the weird sounds that people have heard up there, and he seemed really into it. Now that he can roam about the school, the attic seems like a place he'd explore."

They passed through a crowd of students heading for auditions. Cordelia knew most of them by sight if not by name. She smiled at Brandon Peake, an agreeable boy who she sometimes sat with on the bus. Brandon gave her a friendly wave in return, totally unaware that an old woman wearing a hospital gown was standing right behind him.

"The attic's locked," Benji said.

"Not to the boy," replied Cordelia.

"I was talking about us."

Cordelia grinned. "Don't worry. I have a plan."

"That's exactly why I *should* worry," Benji said.

The copier was in a tiny room that also housed a laminating machine, spools of colored paper for bulletin boards, and a paper cutter armed with a long sharp blade. A massive wrought-iron clock with roman numerals covered the far wall. Its ticking only emphasized their need for haste.

Cordelia knelt in front of the copier and unzipped her bookbag while Benji watched the hall for teachers. The room was off-limits to students unless you had special permission.

"You going to tell me what you're doing?" Benji asked.

"Nope," Cordelia said. "You'll only try to talk me out of it." From her bag she removed a short stack of paper taken from her family's printer. Each sheet had been carefully crumpled and torn. Cordelia placed the entire pile in the copier tray, set the number of copies to fifty, and pressed the Copy key. In just a few seconds, the copier began to emit strange noises as deep within its inner workings paper crumpled and jammed. All sorts of lights began to flash. Cordelia reopened the tray, grabbed the remaining doctored sheets, and tossed them into the recycling bin. She didn't want anyone figuring out that the copier had been jammed intentionally.

"Why?" Benji asked, his face aghast.

"Three minutes until Mrs. Machen gets here," Cordelia said, checking the clock. "We have to get to the main office and wait. When Mrs. Machen sees that the copier is broken, that's where she'll go. Mrs. Flippin is the only one who can fix it. It'll just be her in the office this time of day. When she goes upstairs, we'll take the extra set of keys in her desk drawer."

"I don't know, Cord," Benji said. "Sneaking around after school is one thing. Stealing keys—"

"Borrowing."

"—is another."

"It's just half an hour," Cordelia said. "Not even. We'll have them back before she even knows they're missing."

Benji didn't look reassured. "If we get caught, just promise you'll send my spirit into the Bright," he said. "Because my parents *will* kill me."

They found a spot where they could watch the office door without being seen, and waited. Ten minutes later, Mrs. Machen stormed into the office. When she came back, it was with Mrs. Flippin, an older receptionist who somehow knew the name of every student and always had a kind word for everyone.

As soon as the adults were out of sight, Benji and Cordelia slipped into the office and snagged the keys. They were on a little ring with a photo of Mrs. Flippin's adorable grandkids, which made Cordelia feel guiltier than anything else she had done.

They ran up the stairs.

Compared to the rest of the school, the fourth floor's appearance was relatively simple. The walls were painted white, the wooden floors unpolished. The only adornment were the mirrors that lined both sides of the hall. These varied in size and shape, though most had gilded frames. A number of mirrors were concealed by long black curtains, as though a vampire were coming to visit.

"I wonder why some of them are covered up," Cordelia said.

"It's to protect us," Benji replied, as though the answer were obvious. "No one ever told you?"

"Told me what?"

Benji lowered his voice to a whisper. "If you see your reflection in one of the covered mirrors, it means you're going to die."

Cordelia felt her stomach clench. Just a few weeks ago she had peeked beneath one of the black curtains. *I remember thinking how clear my reflection was*, she thought.

Benji burst into laughter.

"You made that up, didn't you?" Cordelia asked.

"Just because you believe in ghosts doesn't mean you have to believe in everything!"

"Good advice," Cordelia said. "Also, I hate you."

There was only one way to get to the attic: a dimly lit set of stairs that squeaked beneath their feet. The door at the top was charred at its corners. A yellowed sign warned any potential trespassers of the dangerous conditions beyond this point.

"You sure about this?" Benji asked. "They don't put signs like that up without a good reason."

"Let's at least take a look. If it seems too dangerous, like we're going to fall through the floor or something, we'll come right—"

"Shh," Benji said, holding a finger to his lips. "You hear that?"

Cordelia listened. Behind the attic door she heard the flicker and whoosh of flames. She placed her palm flat against the door and quickly withdrew it.

"It's hot," she whispered. "Just like Mason said."

"I don't know about this," Benji said. "What if Elijah Shadow is waiting in there for us?"

"So what?" Cordelia asked. "We've met loads of ghosts before."

"Something tells me this is going to be different," Benji said.

There were at least twenty keys on Mrs. Flippin's key ring. Benji found the winner on the very first try.

It's almost like something inside can't wait for us to enter, Cordelia thought.

They opened the door.

The Attic

They stood in silence, too stunned to speak. Cordelia blinked several times in rapid succession, wondering if her eyes were playing tricks on her.

"Umm," Benji said. "Are you seeing this?"

"Seeing—yes. Believing? No."

The attic was *nice*. It looked more like a posh apartment than the top floor of a haunted school: hardwood floors, brightly painted walls, chic furniture. There wasn't a hint of fire damage.

"I don't get it," Benji said. "This place should be falling apart."

"Someone must have fixed it up." Cordelia started to close the door and saw a metal box hanging from the other side. "What's this thing?"

Benji touched it with his fingertips and jerked back his hand.

"It's a heater," he said, blowing on his fingers. "That's why the door's hot. I wonder . . ." He took a single step out of the apartment. Cordelia heard the roar of flames behind her. They were coming from a large speaker hanging from the wall.

"There must be some kind of sensor," Benji said as he closed the door behind him. "Like those houses at Halloween that make creepy sounds when you go trick-or-treating."

"The attic isn't haunted at all," Cordelia said.

She searched the living room, wondering what it all meant. The furniture was clean, the floor immaculate. Even the curtains looked ironed. Several paintings hung from the wall, mostly landscapes. Cordelia recognized one of them from a book of famous artists she owned, though she couldn't remember the painter's name.

"Does someone *live* here?" Benji asked.

"It sure looks like it. That's probably why they worked so hard to scare people away. They don't want anyone poking into their business."

She passed beneath the archway on the other side of the room and entered a fully functional kitchen. There were a few dishes neatly stacked in the sink and a bowl of fresh fruit on the counter.

"We should go," Benji said. "I don't like this."

Cordelia shook her head. "We need to find out who lives here," she insisted. "If they're trying to keep people away, it means they have something to hide. It's probably the same person who locked me in the boiler room."

"Exactly!" Benji said. "They're dangerous! And they're not going to be happy if they come home and find us."

"Then we better make it quick. Let's start in the living room. Look for—I don't know. Photos? Mail? Anything that will help us figure out—"

The fake flames whooshed to life, making both of them jump. A key slid into the lock. The doorknob turned. Cordelia, frozen in fear, would have stood there until the front door opened if Benji hadn't yanked her down the hallway. They dove into a tiny bedroom with nowhere to hide.

Cordelia heard the door shut.

We're trapped, she thought.

Fortunately, the footsteps were headed away from them, toward the kitchen. Cordelia heard running water. Using the sound as cover, they crept out of the bedroom to a door at the end of the hall. It opened onto a vast area that looked more like a proper attic, with plywood flooring and a sloped ceiling. In addition to antique school desks, standalone chalkboards, and enough overhead projectors for the entire state of New Hampshire, dozens of massive dollhouses sat atop white pedestals. They varied greatly in style, from a simple ranch with a white picket fence to what appeared to be some kind of castle.

Benji met Cordelia's eyes and shook his head: *I don't want to go in there! No way!*

She shrugged: *What choice do we have?*

In the kitchen, the sound of running water came to an abrupt stop. Cordelia shoved Benji into the attic and closed the door behind them, cutting off the light from the hallway and plunging them into an even deeper darkness. They searched for a good hiding place, Cordelia wincing at every creaking floorboard. At one point she thought she heard footsteps and turned quickly, knocking over a dusty globe with her elbow. Benji caught it before it hit the floor.

"Careful," he whispered.

They settled behind a table propped on one side. The pedestal next to them bore a stone farmhouse that filled Cordelia with a vague sense of unease. The level of detail was awe inspiring. Individual stones had been painstakingly slotted into place, and each window was made from real glass. Cordelia could even see a tiny keyhole in the front door.

It looks totally different from Shadow School, she thought. *But for some reason it reminds me of it just the same.*

With a burst of insight, she grabbed Benji's shoulder and whispered in his ear.

"They're not dollhouses!"

Before Cordelia could explain further, the attic door swung open. Dr. Roqueni stood there, framed by a rectangle of light. She didn't look happy.

Not her, Cordelia thought, feeling a stab of betrayal. Benji pulled her behind the table and held a finger to his lips.

"I know you're here, Cordelia," Dr. Roqueni said. She entered the attic but left the door open behind her. "Are Benji and Agnes with you? No matter. You can all come out now. I'm not going to hurt you."

Cordelia and Benji remained still. Their hiding place was deep in the shadows, beyond the reach of the hallway light spilling across the attic.

"I apologize for locking you in the boiler room," Dr. Roqueni said, checking beneath a desk. "I came back to open the door, but you had already found your way out through the hidden passageway—which I have since sealed up, incidentally, so no more snooping. You were never in any real danger. I just wanted to scare some sense into you so you'd stop freeing the ghosts."

Dr. Roqueni was getting closer. It was only a matter of time before she found them. *I'll distract her*, Cordelia mouthed to Benji. *You get help.* Benji shook his head.

"I realize now that I should have told you the truth from the beginning," Dr. Roqueni continued. "Would you like to know why Shadow School has so many ghosts? After his beloved wife died, Elijah dedicated himself to the study of haunted houses." She paused a moment to straighten a hanging windowpane on a Tudor-style house. "He made these models of them with his own two hands. You see, Shadow School was designed to be a—"

"Haunted house," Cordelia said, ignoring Benji's objections and stepping out of their hiding place. "It's called archimancy. Mr. Derleth already told me all about it."

As Cordelia talked, she moved toward the opposite end of the attic. Dr. Roqueni carefully followed her progress. *Keep looking this way*, thought Cordelia. *That will give Benji a chance to escape.*

"Our newest faculty member sure has a keen interest in local history," Dr. Roqueni said, stepping to her left and cutting off Cordelia's most direct path to the exit. "But I doubt he knows the whole truth. After Elijah built Shadow School, he invited the most prominent psychics and paranormal experts from around the world to live here. Most of them shared Elijah's vision. They longed to learn more about the mysteries of life after death and maybe bring comfort to those grieving over their loved ones." Her expression grew dark. "But there were others with far less noble ideas about how the dead could be used. Profit. Revenge. Power. Elijah decided that archimancy was too dangerous and set fire to his office, destroying all his journals and blueprints. Only something went wrong, and Elijah got trapped in the room as well. He died protecting his secrets."

"The attic seems fine now," Cordelia said.

"It was repaired in secret," Dr. Roqueni said. "We needed a place to watch over the school without being disturbed."

"We?"

Dr. Roqueni raised her chin and fixed Cordelia with a regal look.

"Elijah was my great-great-grandfather," she said. "I'm a Shadow."

Cordelia gasped in surprise: *No wonder she knows so much.* From the corner of her eye, she caught a glimpse of Benji sneaking through the attic. He paused a moment to look back at her with concern and slipped through the door. Cordelia tried to mask her relief.

He'll be back with help soon, she thought. *I just have to keep Dr. Roqueni talking until then.*

Hopefully she could learn some answers.

"Is that why you don't want me to help the ghosts?" Cordelia asked. "So you can study them?"

"Not at all," Dr. Roqueni said, approaching her. "Why don't you come into the living room? I'll make tea and tell you the entire story. I promise you'll feel differently about the ghosts by the time I'm done."

Cordelia slid to her right, trying to keep as much of the attic junk as possible between Dr. Roqueni and herself. She was afraid that the moment she let her guard down, the principal would reach out and grab her.

"Tell me your story first," Cordelia said. "Then I'll decide if I want any tea."

"As you wish," Dr. Roqueni said with just the hint of a smile. "I was twenty-nine when my uncle Darius told me that I was to be the new principal of Shadow School. There were other Shadows all around the world—our family tree has spread wide and far since Elijah's days. But I was the only one with the Sight."

"You can see ghosts?" Cordelia asked.

"To a certain extent," Dr. Roqueni replied. "I can't see ghosts in the outside world—that's a rare gift indeed—but I have just enough talent to see the ones in Shadow School. The spirits are closer here. Magnified." She shrugged. "But I had no interest in the family business. I had just received my doctorate in art history. I wanted to travel the world, not live in a creepy old school. My mother begged me to help the family, though, and I finally gave in. I figured I'd do it for a year or two, just to make her happy. Then I'd start my real life."

Dr. Roqueni's eyes took on a glazed, faraway look. Cordelia had seen the same expression in her mother's eyes when she talked about her teenage dreams of becoming a dancer: the bittersweet look of what might have been.

"So here I was, stuck in Shadow School, playing caretaker to a bunch of dead people. I was angry, miserable, and bored. Since I didn't have anything better to do, I started watching the spirits. Uncle Darius had warned me not to disturb them—'Just get the living out by nightfall and let that old building do its thing,' as he put it. Thing was, my uncle was five hundred miles away, and I figured I knew a lot more than he did anyway, with my fancy college education. I noticed how all the ghosts seemed to be seeking some sort of personal object. Their appearance provided a careful observer all the clues she needed. Sound familiar?"

"We call them Brightkeys," Cordelia said.

"That's lovely," Dr. Roqueni said with a genuine smile, and despite everything Cordelia blushed at the compliment. "Not even Elijah could explain why the ghosts offered clues to their own salvation, incidentally.

I've always believed that some entity, one with a sense of fair play, learned how Elijah had corrupted the natural order and intervened. In any case, one night I gave this barefoot little ghost a new pair of shoes, just to see what would happen. Lo and behold, she vanished into the light. That felt good, let me tell you. I was helping the dead move on from a terrible, lonely existence. What could possibly be wrong with that?"

Dr. Roqueni gazed out a dormer window, lost in her story. Cordelia inched closer to the exit.

"I soon learned that I wasn't the only one at Shadow School who could see the ghosts," Dr. Roqueni said, her back facing Cordelia now. "A man named David Fisher had the Sight as well. We worked together to free as many ghosts as we could, never stopping to think about the—"

Cordelia took off, nearly colliding with a model of a Gothic manor before bursting through the door and into the hallway of the apartment. Benji was standing in the living room with his hands on his knees.

"Got . . . help," he managed, out of breath. Mr. Ward entered the apartment. Cordelia was usually frightened of the huge custodian, but this time his intimidating presence made her feel safe and secure.

"Why are you here?" Dr. Roqueni asked with a sharp tone.

"The boy begged me to come," Mr. Ward said. "Told me his friend was in trouble."

"Did he tell anyone else?" Dr. Roqueni asked.

Mr. Ward shook his head. "School's empty this time of day," he said.

"That's fortunate," Dr. Roqueni said. "Otherwise we could have had a real problem on our hands."

"My thoughts exactly," Mr. Ward said.

He closed the door and locked it behind him.

18

Cordelia Makes a Decision

Cordelia and Benji sat nervously on the edge of the couch while Dr. Roqueni set the kettle to boil in the kitchen. Mr. Ward leaned against the door with his huge arms crossed, making it clear that there was no point trying to escape.

"You sure it's a good idea to be telling them all this?" Mr. Ward called out to Dr. Roqueni in the kitchen. "What if they tell their parents?"

"Their parents won't believe them," Dr. Roqueni replied over the sound of a screeching tea kettle. "Besides, I wanted to tell them everything as soon as I figured out what they were up to. *You* convinced me it was a better plan to scare them off instead."

"I wasn't sure they would listen," Mr. Ward said with a defensive tone. "It's the helpful types who always have the biggest stubborn streaks." A mournful look softened his features. "Just like Dave."

Is he talking about David Fisher? Cordelia wondered, remembering the horrible rumor about what Mr. Ward had done to the custodian. *Is he going to do the same thing to us?*

The fear must have been evident on her face, because Mr. Ward shook his head in disgust.

"I know what people say," he grumbled. "I chopped up his body and tossed the pieces in the furnace, right? It ain't true. None of it. Dave was my best friend in the world. I never would have hurt him. We argued that last night because—"

Dr. Roqueni re-entered the room with a small serving tray holding a teapot and three cups.

"That's enough, Chris," she said, placing the tray on a coffee table. "None of this will make any sense if I don't start from the beginning." She poured Cordelia a cup of tea and handed it to her. "Chamomile. It'll calm your nerves."

Cordelia took a tiny sip. The tea was hot with a fragrant aroma. She didn't love the taste, but she had to confess that it immediately settled her churning stomach. Dr. Roqueni poured cups for Benji and herself and settled into the love seat opposite them.

"My dad is picking me up soon," Cordelia said. "He'll know something's up if I'm not outside."

"This won't take long," Dr. Roqueni said. "I just need to finish my story."

"And then you're going to let us leave?" Benji asked dubiously.

"Yes," Dr. Roqueni said. "What you do after that is up to you. But I think you'll come to see things my way."

She took a sip of her tea, cradling the cup in both hands for warmth.

"I've left out an important part of my story," she said. "The ghost snatchers. They only come at night. Did you see them?"

Cordelia nodded.

"There are always three," Dr. Roqueni said. "The younger two get replaced from time to time, but their roles remain the same. There's a worker who pushes the cart and sets things up before the other two arrive. That's Lenny, these days. And then a second custodian who hypnotizes the ghosts and makes sure they stay still while the deed is done. We named this one Whistler, for obvious reasons." Dr. Roqueni shifted uncomfortably in her seat. "And finally, there's the leader, the man with the piercing green eyes. He never changes. No one knows what his real name is—or if he's even human, to be honest. The Shadow family has always called him Geist."

"They're awful," Cordelia said. "They hurt the ghosts."

"Yes, they do," Dr. Roqueni said. She looked down into her teacup. "And part of my job as principal of Shadow School is to help them do it."

Cordelia's eyes widened.

"You *help* them?" she asked.

"I make sure the school is empty at night," Dr. Roqueni said. "They like it better that way. I imagine from their perspective the living are like a bunch of gnats flying around—hard to see but still annoying."

"How could you do that?" Cordelia asked, half rising from her seat. "You know how helpless the ghosts are! You should be trying to—"

"There's been an unspoken agreement between the ghost snatchers and Shadows for decades," Dr. Roqueni said in a firm voice. "We leave them alone. They leave us alone."

"But they're hurting the ghosts!" Cordelia exclaimed.

"And *helping* us," Dr. Roqueni said. She leaned forward and poured herself a fresh cup of tea. "The word 'custodian' has multiple meanings. In this case, I mean it in the sense of 'guardian' or 'protector.' As you must have realized by now, new ghosts are always arriving here in Shadow School. Uncle Darius told me that without the ghost snatchers, their numbers might escalate out of control. He wasn't clear about what might happen then, only that it would be extremely dangerous. 'We don't like the ghost snatchers, but they're a necessary evil,' he told me. 'Just like bats keeping a mosquito population under control.'"

"Ghosts aren't mosquitos," Cordelia snapped. "They're people."

"I thought the same thing when I first arrived here," Dr. Roqueni said. "My pity for the trapped spirits who walk these halls overrode my good sense. That's why David and I helped them, despite my uncle's warning. Well, of course the ghost snatchers didn't like that. They're extremely territorial. I should have thought it through first. But I was young and so sure I was doing the right thing." She fixed Cordelia and Benji with a pointed look. "You two know how that is, don't you?"

Cordelia felt her face grow warm.

"Geist warned us first," Dr. Roqueni said. "I was awoken by a crash in the middle of the night and found all my furniture flying around the living room. When that didn't scare me off, he used his powers in the cafeteria. It was just like what happened to your grade, only worse, because back then we used hard plastic trays and not the foam ones. I stopped freeing the ghosts after that. I wasn't worried about myself. I was worried about the students. But David didn't want to stop. He felt that being able to see the ghosts imparted a certain duty."

"I tried to talk him out of it," Mr. Ward added with a regretful look, "but both of us have a short fuse, so we just ended up screaming at each other. That was the last time I ever saw him."

Using this new information, Cordelia reconsidered the rumors she had heard about the custodian. The two men argued, just like everyone said, but not because Mr. Ward hated David Fisher. It was because he was worried about him.

"Since David's disappearance, I've been a model Shadow," Dr. Roqueni said, straightening. "I gave up my childish dreams and dedicated myself to keeping the ghost snatchers happy. And that was working out just fine—until you two came along."

Benji hung his head.

"I don't want anyone getting hurt because of something we did," he said.

"But I don't want to stop saving the ghosts, either!" Cordelia exclaimed. "Why should they have to suffer? There must be a way to stop the ghost snatchers!"

"There's not," Dr. Roqueni said. "All we can do is give them what they want so they don't harm the living."

"Well, that *stinks*!" Cordelia exclaimed.

The worst part was she could see Dr. Roqueni's point. Logically speaking, it made more sense to value the living than the dead, and if she kept helping the ghosts, someone at Shadow School was going to get hurt—or vanish.

But if I don't help the ghosts, they'll never find their Brights, Cordelia thought. *They'll be sitting ducks until the ghost snatchers get them.*

Cordelia thought of the boy, still lost or hiding somewhere in the school. How could she just abandon him?

"I appreciate your position, Cordelia," Dr. Roqueni said. "You've come to care for the spirits of Shadow School. Your feelings do you credit. You are, however, only eleven, and not used to dealing with such difficult decisions, so allow me to make it simpler. My family might not be as wealthy as they used to be, but they still have connections. You said your father lost his job in San Francisco, correct? That's why you had to move?"

"So what?" Cordelia asked.

"What if I told you that just a few words whispered in the right ear could get his old job back? Or a better job? Imagine that. You could move back to California and leave this place forever."

The offer, so sudden and unexpected, staggered Cordelia.

"You could do that?" she asked.

"All it would take is a single phone call," Dr. Roqueni said. She flashed a smile at Benji. "I'm sure I could do something to help your family as well. Your parents work so hard, and then there are your little sisters to think about. Don't they deserve—"

"Leave my family out of this," Benji said, with a sharpness to his tone that Cordelia had never heard before.

"As you wish," Dr. Roqueni said. "However, you should also know that if you ignore me and free even one more ghost, I will be forced to place a phone call to a different branch of the Shadow family. In this particular scenario, the consequences for you and your loved ones will not be pleasant. Jobs can be lost, mortgages foreclosed. I would hate to do that. But if you won't listen to reason—what choice do I have?"

If Dr. Roqueni was truly reluctant to make such a phone call, Cordelia doubted it was because she had their best interests at heart. Rather, she suspected the call would be viewed by the other Shadows as a failure on Dr. Roqueni's part, an admission that she couldn't handle things on her own.

"I won't go near the ghosts again," Benji said.

"Cordelia?" Dr. Roqueni asked.

"Fine," she hissed through clenched teeth.

"Then it's settled," Dr. Roqueni said, clapping her hands together. "I'm glad you two have come to your senses. That makes everything so much easier." She nodded to Mr. Ward, who opened the front door. "I'm sure your parents are waiting outside by this point, so you'd better go before they start wondering where you are."

Cordelia was about to exit the apartment when she turned back with one last question.

"What *happened* to David Fisher, anyway?"

Dr. Roqueni shared a look with Mr. Ward.

"That's one mystery that we try not to dwell upon, though we have a few guesses." Dr. Roqueni's face darkened. "If you really want to know, keep freeing the ghosts. You'll find out what happened to David Fisher in no time at all."

fingers passed through her wrist, leaving behind a cold patch of skin. It was like being bitten by an ice spider. Cordelia ignored the pain and continued to stumble backward, windmilling her arms in order to maintain some semblance of balance. If she could only reach the end of the girl's ghost zone—the invisible barrier that tethered each spirit to a specific area of Shadow School—Cordelia knew she would be safe.

"Behind you!" Benji exclaimed.

Cordelia grunted, more in surprise than pain, as her backside collided with something solid. At first she thought it was the wall of the attic. Then she heard a loud crash and realized that she had knocked one of Elijah Shadow's architectural models off its pedestal.

Great, Cordelia thought. If this ghost doesn't kill me, Dr. Roqueni will.

The trick-or-treater stopped less than a foot from Cordelia and pounded her tiny fists against invisible walls. The witch mask hung askew on her face, revealing a pale white chin and bloodless lips.

"I'm so sorry," Cordelia said, too ashamed to meet the girl's eyes. "This is our fault."

Benji scooped up the pile of miniature chocolates and approached the ghost. Cordelia waved him away, worried that the girl would redirect her anger now that Cordelia was beyond her reach, but Benji ignored her.

The girl turned to face him.

"I'm sorry, too," he said, and dropped all the chocolates into the trick-or-treater's plastic pumpkin. Her Bright appeared instantly, a crisp autumn evening buzzing with laughter and doorbells.

The girl graced Benji and Cordelia with a smile of forgiveness and left the world of the living forever.

"How bad did she get you?" Benji asked, gently lifting her wrist. Cordelia met his deep brown eyes, soft with concern, and decided that she was no longer annoyed with him.

"Not as bad as I deserve," she said. "I'll be fine." She looked down at the house that she had knocked from its pedestal. "Maybe."

GET CAUGHT UP IN
THE THICKETY

BOOK 1

BOOK 2

BOOK 3

BOOK 4

Read them all!

★ "Absolutely thrilling."—*Publishers Weekly* (starred review)

★ "Spellbinding."—*Kirkus Reviews* (starred review)

19

The Difference Between Them

They found the boy four days later. He was hiding in the reference section of the library, couched behind a corner bookshelf packed with dusty encyclopedias. The moment she saw him, a heavy weight leaped off Cordelia's chest. She had begun to fear the worst.

"Hey there," Cordelia said. She pressed her head against the wall, trying to get a closer look, but it was dark behind the shelf, and the boy was backed against the corner. "You can come out now. It's safe."

The boy turned away from her.

"Did we find him?" Agnes asked Benji, keeping her voice as quiet as possible. The other students in the

193

library were already giving them curious looks.

"We found him," Benji said.

"Then why aren't we high-fiving each other?" Agnes asked.

"Something's wrong," Cordelia said, wishing more than ever that she knew the boy's name so she could call to him. "Won't you please come out?"

The boy shook his head.

"I can't help you if I don't know what's wrong," Cordelia said. "Besides, I thought we were friends."

The boy closed his eyes for a few moments, then took a step through the bookshelf and into the light. Cordelia clapped a hand to her mouth.

She could see straight through his body.

"What is it?" Agnes whispered. She looked frustrated and a little annoyed, as though Cordelia and Benji were having a conversation in a language she didn't speak. "What's going on?"

"He's not as solid as he used to be," Benji said.

Cordelia got down to one knee so she could be eye level with the boy. She wished she could wrap him in her arms.

"Did the men with the cart find you?"

The boy nodded.

"Did it hurt?"

He nodded again.

"I'm sorry I didn't stop them," Cordelia said. She scanned the library to make sure that Dr. Roqueni was nowhere in sight and then added, "But we're going to get you out of this school and where you're meant to be," she whispered. "I promise."

It was unseasonably warm for January—at least by New Hampshire standards—so recess was outside that day. Cordelia was headed toward the playground to meet Benji and Agnes when Francesca Calvino caught up with her and asked if she wanted to play four square on the blacktop. Cordelia had been lab partners with Francesca a few times, and they had gotten along well.

"Sorry," Cordelia said. "I promised Benji and Agnes we'd hang out."

"Can I tag along?" Francesca asked with a smile.

Cordelia cleared her throat awkwardly.

"It kind of just needs to be the three of us today," she said. "Another time?"

"Sure," Francesca said, jamming her hands into her pockets before heading toward the blacktop. Cordelia watched her walk away with a guilty feeling in the pit of her stomach. She hoped she hadn't hurt Francesca's feelings.

This would never happen if I was back in San Francisco, Cordelia thought. *I could be friends with whoever I wanted and not worry about anything more complicated than passing math. And it can happen! All I have to do is ignore the ghosts.*

It would be so easy. But even at eleven, Cordelia knew that the easy choices were seldom the right ones.

There must be another way.

Benji and Agnes were waiting for her on the swings. Cordelia scanned the area for potential eavesdroppers and then hopped up on the swing next to Benji. She had forgotten her gloves, and the chains were like icicles beneath her fingers.

"We have to figure out the boy's Brightkey before it's too late," she said.

"But you've already tried everything," Benji said.

"Obviously not," Cordelia said. "I should start over from the beginning and be more methodical this time. Write things down. Make sure I don't repeat myself." She smiled at Agnes. "Like a scientist."

"That's a good idea," Agnes said. "But aren't we forgetting something? Dr. Roqueni said there would be consequences if you freed any more ghosts."

"We should be okay as long as she doesn't see us," Cordelia said. "When the boy vanishes, she'll just assume the snatchers got him."

"I don't think Dr. Roqueni is our main concern," Agnes said. "What if sending the boy to his Bright gets the ghost snatchers mad? There might be another incident like the one in the lunchroom. Or they might go after you like they did with David Fisher!"

"The boy doesn't have a lot of time left," Cordelia said. "We have to risk it."

Agnes turned to face her. She was too tall for the swing, and her feet dragged across the ground.

"I know it sounds harsh," she said in a hesitant voice, "but ghosts aren't meant to be in the living world. What if Dr. Roqueni's uncle is right, and the snatchers are actually fulfilling an important function? Like—I don't know—white blood cells that kill infections? It might be best to stay out of their way and let nature take its course."

Cordelia couldn't believe what she was hearing.

"So we should just *let* them take the boy?"

"Maybe it only seems bad," Agnes said. "We have no idea what happens after the ghosts vanish. For all we know, they go to their Brights!"

Cordelia's cheeks, already flushed, grew redder still. Fear and frustration amplified her anger.

"That is the single dumbest thing I've ever heard!" she exclaimed. "There's no way that the snatchers are sending ghosts to—"

"Chill, Cord," Benji cut in, holding his hands up in a placating gesture. "We're all on the same team here." He turned to Agnes, who looked flustered. "I know you're just trying to help, but trust me on this one: the ghost snatchers aren't here to do anything good. My guess is that when they're done peeling a ghost, it simply disappears altogether. No Bright for them. No anything. Which is kind of awful."

"Exactly," Cordelia said.

"But," Benji said, spinning in her direction, "I do see Agnes's point. All this trouble with the snatchers began because we messed around with the way Shadow School works. I want to help the boy—and the other ghosts too—but we need to be smart about this. Maybe there's another solution we haven't thought of yet."

"There's not enough time," Cordelia said. "We need to save him!"

"You *can't* save him," Agnes snapped. "He's already dead."

Until this point, Cordelia had managed to rein in her temper, but now it broke free of its shackles with a vengeance. She hopped off the swing and jabbed her index finger in Agnes's face.

"You wouldn't say that if you could see him! But you can't. You can't see *any* of them! So why are you even part of this conversation? You don't belong here!"

Agnes looked stunned but not surprised, as though Cordelia were confirming a long-held suspicion. Tears streamed from her eyes.

198

"I'm sorry," Agnes said. "I wish I could see them like you can. I don't know why I can't!"

Cordelia said nothing. Her outburst had popped her anger like a balloon, leaving behind nothing but a cold, mean feeling. She knew she should apologize. But she also knew she was right. To Agnes, this had always been a kind of science experiment. The ghosts weren't real to her. She couldn't see how lost they were, how helpless. She couldn't see the fear in the boy's eyes—as real as any living child.

"Cordelia?" Agnes asked in a pleading tone.

Cordelia stared down at the ground, not knowing what to say. After a few moments, Agnes ran off. Her empty swing rocked back and forth for a while and then finally came to a stop.

20

Room 314

Cordelia went to the library every morning to visit the boy. He seemed happy to see her, though his smile now possessed a bittersweet quality, as though he knew their time together would soon be coming to a close. Although the boy hesitantly came out of his hiding spot when Cordelia arrived, he was too frightened to leave the library. Any loud noise—the morning bell, a dropped book—would send him scurrying back behind the shelf.

If the ghost snatchers find him again, he's done for, Cordelia thought. For the first time in her life, she felt the suffocating pressure of having someone else totally depend on her. The thought that she might fail the boy was scarier than anything else in Shadow School.

Despite Dr. Roqueni's warning, Cordelia hadn't given up trying to figure out the boy's Brightkey. *Glasses. Pajamas. Trains.* She repeated the clues as she lay in bed each night, hoping this mantra would blossom into a solution while she slept.

Agnes would have a better chance figuring it out, she thought.

Unfortunately, the two girls hadn't spoken since their falling out. Benji thought they were both being stubborn and unreasonable. Since they refused to be in each other's presence, he had to divide his time between them.

"I feel like the child of divorced parents," Benji whispered to Cordelia during social studies. "Agnes made me a schedule. I'm having lunch with you on Monday and Wednesday, and with her on Tuesday and Thursday."

"What about Friday?"

"Friday is when I make a bunch of new friends to replace the old ones who are acting like idiots."

"Don't be mean."

"Enough chatter, you two," Mr. Derleth said. "Get back to work."

"Sorry," Cordelia said, and returned to researching the dangers of overpopulation. Usually Mr. Derleth was pretty chill about letting the class talk when they were working on projects, but he had been uncharacteristically irritable of late. Cordelia thought he seemed particularly annoyed at her for some reason.

Not annoyed, she amended. *Disappointed. But I have one of the highest grades in the class. What could I have done to disappoint him?*

The bell rang.

"Did you see that they got the man in the gray suit?" Benji asked as they left the room.

"No!" Cordelia exclaimed. "Are you sure?"

"Positive."

Waving to the man in his window every morning had become something of a routine for Cordelia as she entered Shadow School. *But I didn't wave today*, she thought sadly. *I didn't even look up. It's almost like I knew.* The worst part was that she had a great idea about what the man's Brightkey might be, but the threat of reprisal from the ghost snatchers had kept her from using it. Now that chance was lost forever.

"Don't take it so hard," Benji said, noting her slumped shoulders and crestfallen expression. "There's nothing we could have done."

"Actually, there was. Only we didn't do it."

Agnes brushed past them, dragging her rolling backpack. She didn't even look in Cordelia's direction.

"Will you *please* talk to her?" Benji asked.

"It's not my fault she's being so stubborn," Cordelia said. "And, yeah, I could have been nicer about it, but I wasn't wrong. We can see ghosts. She can't. That makes us different."

"So we can't be friends with people who are different than us?"

"That's not what I—"

"Bummer. Because I'm Peruvian and you're half-Chinese. Guess this friendship's over."

"It's not the same and you know it! Agnes will never understand how much the ghosts need our help if she can't see them!"

"You're right," Benji said.

Cordelia looked at him in surprise. "I am?"

"Totally," Benji said. "Agnes can't possibly understand what's going on at Shadow School like we do. It wouldn't be fair to expect her to. What has she really seen? A few flickering lights when a ghost goes into its Bright? Certainly not enough to convince her there's a ghost in every corner. And let's not forget the way that Agnes's mind works. She's a scientist at heart. That girl lives on proof. And yet . . . she's still been helping us for months. Have you thought about what that must be like from her perspective? We're doing this because we can see the ghosts with our own two eyes. But Agnes?

The only thing that she has to go by is her total and complete faith in you." He leaned forward and gazed intently into Cordelia's eyes. "Does that sound like the kind of friendship you want to just throw away?"

Cordelia suddenly felt very small. *If another girl told me she saw ghosts and asked for my help, would I dive right in like Agnes did?* Cordelia doubted it. Doing so would take a level of trust that she just didn't possess.

What have I done? she thought.

Cordelia intended to apologize at lunch the next day, but Agnes was nowhere to be found. Benji suggested she try the third floor. Apparently, Agnes had some sort of secret thinking spot up there.

I had no idea, Cordelia thought. *Some friend I am.*

After a long search, she finally found Agnes sitting on the floor of room 314, looking up at an old-fashioned chalkboard with grim determination. Cordelia immediately knew what she was trying to do and felt her heart break.

"Why are you here?" Agnes asked when Cordelia entered. She started to rise, her cheeks flushed with embarrassment.

"Just give me three minutes," Cordelia said, closing the door behind her. "After that, I promise I won't ever bother you again."

Agnes still looked dubious, but she sat back down.

"Here," Cordelia said, handing her the brown paper bag in her hands. "This really smart girl once told me that if you want to be someone's friend, you bake them a treat. It shows you mean business."

Agnes opened up the bag and peeked inside.

"You made me a brownie," she said.

"With walnuts," Cordelia said. "Can I sit next to you?"

Agnes didn't say no. Cordelia figured this was good enough and took a seat. She nodded toward the blackboard.

"How long have you been trying to see him?" Cordelia asked.

Agnes started to deny it, then realized there was no point. "Since just after Halloween," she said. "I figured that maybe seeing ghosts was like looking at a stereogram. You know, one of those pictures that appears two-dimensional at first, only if you stare at it long enough and in the right way these hidden images pop out."

"I know what you're talking about," Cordelia said. "My mom has this old book filled with them. It's called *Magic Eye*."

"Exactly," Agnes said. "So I looked at the list you and Benji made and picked a ghost that would be good to practice on. No one comes up here this time of day, so I knew I wouldn't be disturbed. Besides, the way you described him: 'an old man who looks like a clown out of his make-up.' I really wanted to see for myself."

"Those are Benji's words, not mine. He's actually a better writer than he thinks he is."

"I noticed that too. He's modest about it."

"He tends to be modest about everything except soccer."

"And his hair," Agnes said. "That boy *loves* his hair."

The two girls laughed, and the rift between them broke like a curse. Agnes took out the brownie that Cordelia had made and offered her half.

"Thanks," Cordelia said, taking a bite. It wasn't as good as Agnes's, but it was still a brownie.

"I thought I saw a kind of blur a few days ago, but it was probably just my imagination," Agnes said, still staring at the front of the room. Her cheeks burned. "I want to see them so badly. That was the plan, you know. Come back to you all triumphant. 'Now I can see ghosts too!' And then you would like me again. So stupid."

Cordelia put her head on Agnes's shoulder.

"I like you whether you can see ghosts or not," she said. "You're my best friend. That won't change even if we never talk about ghosts again."

"That's too bad," Agnes said with a wicked smile. "Because I may have figured out how to get rid of the ghost snatchers for good."

Cordelia sat up.

"For real?" she asked.

"Absolutely," Agnes said. "I'm not saying it will definitely work, but it's something."

"Well, something is better than nothing," Cordelia said, pulling Agnes to her feet. "Let's find Benji. He'll want to hear your idea too."

As they left, Agnes paused and took one last look at the front of the room. "Do you really think I can train myself to see ghosts?"

"Why not? Stranger things have happened."

Cordelia didn't have the heart to tell Agnes that they had already sent this ghost to its Bright but forgotten to update the list. For months now, Agnes had been staring at an ordinary blackboard.

At gym, Benji complained of a sore ankle while Cordelia and Agnes claimed that they had forgotten their sneakers. Mr. Bruce shook his head in annoyance and banished them all to the bleachers, just as they'd hoped he would. Agnes and Benji immediately climbed to the top row, but Cordelia paused to take a long look behind the bleachers. There was nothing back there but dust and a couple of water bottles that had slipped through the cracks.

Was it really only September when I first saw the boy? she thought in disbelief. *It feels like years.*

She joined her friends while the rest of the class played volleyball. Mr. Bruce was wearing a bright yellow jersey emblazoned with *Sakai Blazers*—the name of a Japanese volleyball team—but despite his enthusiasm for the sport, the students barely exerted any effort at all. It was the last block of the day, and everyone just wanted to go home.

"So what's this genius idea of yours, Ag?" Benji asked, rubbing his hands together.

"Don't get too excited," Agnes replied. "I don't even know if it's possible. And we would need Mr. Ward's help to build it."

"Build what?" Cordelia asked.

"A ghost trap."

Cordelia tried to mask her disappointment. The last thing she wanted to do was hurt Agnes's feelings again.

"That's an interesting idea," Cordelia said, picking at her sleeve. "It's just, um—"

"You can't trap something that can pass through walls," Benji said.

Cordelia expected Agnes to blush and stammer, but instead she smiled with surprising confidence.

"The ghosts can pass through *some* walls," Agnes said. "Not all. Otherwise they'd be able to leave Shadow School."

"True," Cordelia said. "But I don't understand how that helps us."

"It proves they can be trapped," Agnes said. "All we have to do is build the right sort of cage."

"And how are we going to do that?"

The bleachers creaked as Agnes rocked back and forth in her seat. There was a feverish excitement in her eyes. "Remember how Elijah Shadow made his money? He had these private shows where rich people paid to see ghosts up close and personal. It only worked for those with the Sight, but still—that meant he must have captured the ghosts somehow." She looked at Cordelia. "Did Mr. Derleth mention how he did that?"

Cordelia nodded. "He showed me a drawing someone made—a guest at one of the shows. Each ghost was in a"—Cordelia gasped, beginning to see where Agnes was going with this—"in a kind of box."

"A ghost box," Agnes said, grinning. "Elijah must have used archimancy to build them. That's why the ghosts couldn't escape. And if it can hold a ghost . . ."

"It can hold the ghost snatchers," Benji said. He burst into a gigantic smile. "You're a genius!"

"It's just a theory," Agnes said, blushing. "And we

still have to *build* them. Maybe it's a lot harder than it seems. Maybe it requires material that we don't have access to. I have no idea. But I'd love to at least give it a shot. All we need are the original blueprints, which I'm sure are somewhere in the school."

Cordelia and Benji exchanged a look.

"What?" Agnes asked.

"Dr. Roqueni told us that all of Elijah Shadow's work was destroyed in the attic fire," Cordelia said. "There are no blueprints."

Agnes's face fell. "You never told me."

"I'm sorry," Cordelia said. "It never occurred to me that it might be so important."

They sat in silence and watched their classmates play volleyball. *Another dead end*, Cordelia thought, trying to fight her disappointment. Below her, Mason lost his temper and spiked the ball with his fist. It smacked a smaller boy named Brian Haas in the face, knocking him to the floor. Mr. Bruce ran over to check on the injured student while Mason and his cronies tried to control their laughter.

"There must be a hundred rooms in Shadow School," Agnes said, mostly to herself. "Who would put their office all the way in the attic?"

"Maybe he wanted to be left alone," Benji suggested.

"Elijah and his daughter were the only ones living here," Agnes said. "How much more privacy did he need? Besides, Elijah was an old man by this point. Why climb up and down those stairs if he didn't have to? It would make a lot more sense if his office was on one of the lower floors."

"Maybe he stored his work in the attic but had his office somewhere else," Benji suggested.

They batted this idea around and came to the conclusion that the attic was the *last* place Elijah Shadow would store his blueprints. Attics were hot in the summer, cold in the winter, and home to mice all year round. That made them a perfectly adequate place to store Christmas decorations and old toys you didn't play with anymore—not your life's work.

"There's a photo of his office on the first floor," Cordelia said. "Let's check it out and see if we're missing something."

The moment class ended, the trio dashed through the halls to the large black-and-white photograph of Elijah Shadow hanging on the wall. For the first time, Cordelia ignored the architect working at his drafting table and instead focused on the office around him. Towering bookcases packed with leather-bound volumes rose so high that a ladder would be required to

211

reach the upper shelves. There was a simple cot in the corner and two wooden cabinets with wide, shallow drawers.

"There," Cordelia said, pointing at the cabinets. "They had something like those at my library back in California. It was where they kept these cool old maps."

"Those kinds of drawers would work for blueprints too," Benji said. "That must be where he stored them."

"But this doesn't look anything like the attic," Cordelia said, studying the photograph. "The ceiling is way too high—and not slanted. In fact, I don't recognize this room at all." She turned to the others. "Does it look familiar to you?"

Agnes and Benji shook their heads.

"There aren't any windows," Agnes observed.

"Huh," Cordelia said, standing on her tiptoes as she took a closer look. "That's really weird. An architect would be hunched over his table all day, trying to get each detail exactly right. Wouldn't he want big windows, so he'd have a lot of natural light?"

"Unless it was more important to Elijah that his office remain hidden," Benji suggested. "Since there're no windows, the office might be behind a wall, where no one could ever find it. Remember what Dr. Roqueni said about people wanting to use archimancy for bad things? Elijah wouldn't want his secrets to fall into the wrong hands."

"But if that's the case, it makes even more sense that he destroyed all the blueprints in a fire," Agnes said with a defeated expression. "We're back to the beginning."

Cordelia stared at Elijah Shadow, trying to get a sense of the man across the ocean of years.

"Destroying the blueprints definitely makes the most logical sense," she said. "But that doesn't mean he did it. Look at his eyes. I don't see logic there. I see obsession. He dedicated his life to creating archimancy. He wouldn't destroy everything he did, no matter how dangerous it was. But maybe—he could have pretended to. Let's say everyone thought his real office was in the attic, and it got destroyed in a fire—"

"They'd think the plans were destroyed as well," Benji said. "So they wouldn't go looking for them. It would have been just as good as destroying them for real!"

"But Elijah *died*," Agnes said. "That couldn't have been part of his plan."

"Something must have gone wrong," Cordelia said.

"I don't know," Agnes said, unconvinced. "We're

guessing at things that happened a long, long time ago. We won't know anything until we see this office. And we have no idea where it could be."

"True," Cordelia said. "But I know someone who can find it for us."

21

The Missing Petals

Cordelia needed to get to school early the next morning, so for the first time in weeks she asked her father for a ride. He eagerly agreed. On the way there, they stopped for donuts and hot chocolate at a local bakery. Cordelia was tempted to eat her breakfast while sitting in the passenger seat, but her dad was fastidious about his car, and she didn't want to get crumbs everywhere.

"I've missed our morning drives," Mr. Liu said.

"Me too," Cordelia said. "And not just because of the baked goods."

"Though they help."

"Maybe," Cordelia said. She saw that her father was

wearing the tie she had gotten him for his birthday and smiled. "How do you like your new job?"

Mr. Liu chuckled.

"What?" Cordelia asked.

"I've been at my job for half a year now, Cordy. It's not exactly new anymore."

"Sorry," Cordelia said, looking down at her lap. "Guess I should have asked before."

"You're asking now. That's all that matters." Mr. Liu stopped at a red light. "It's not as exciting as what I did back in San Francisco. But the people are nice, and that counts for a lot. The company has this huge picnic in the summer for employees and their families."

"Sounds like fun," Cordelia said, and was surprised to find that she meant it.

A few minutes later, they made the turn onto the tree-lined road that led up to Shadow School. A thin layer of snow had fallen overnight, and freshly spread salt crunched beneath their tires.

"I've been meaning to ask," Mr. Liu said. "Have you seen any more ghosts?"

Cordelia was so surprised by the question that she nearly spilled her hot chocolate.

"Ghosts? What do you mean?"

"I guess you forgot all about it. The first day of school you told us you saw a ghost in the gym. I was curious if you'd had any other spooky experiences since then. You haven't mentioned anything, but maybe that's because you're afraid we wouldn't believe you."

He sounded genuinely interested—and a little guilty about doubting her in the first place. Nevertheless, Cordelia resisted the urge to tell him the truth. She didn't want to risk her parents actually believing her this time and pulling her out of Shadow School.

"No more ghosts," she said. "Guess it was just my imagination. Creepy old building, you know?"

"Yeah," he said. "Nothing like your old school, right?" Mr. Liu sighed deeply. "I wish we could have stayed in California. It just wasn't in the cards."

"I know, Dad. It's not your fault."

They arrived at the school. Except for a few cars, the parking lot was completely empty. Mr. Liu pulled over to the curb.

"At least it all worked out for the best," he said. "Your mom and I were worried at the beginning, but these last few months? We're never seen you happier."

Cordelia gave him an incredulous look.

"Are you serious?" she asked.

"Of course," Mr. Liu said. "Back in California, you used to spend hours lounging around, looking bored. You complained all the time. Now you seem . . . *driven*. And it's clear how much you adore your new friends.

Your entire face lights up when you talk about them, especially—"

"Don't," Cordelia said, raising her hand. "Mom already gives me enough grief about him."

"Even your grades are better. You're finally taking school seriously."

"Huh," Cordelia said. *Could he be right? Could I actually like it here?* She stared out the passenger-side window at the wall surrounding the school. If she squinted, she could make out the words on the plaque: *Elijah Z. Shadow Middle School. Grades 5–8. Knowledge. Character. Spirit.* It was a dangerous place full of secrets and ghosts. And yet, for some unfathomable reason, she couldn't wait to go inside.

How long have I felt this way?

Cordelia guessed a long time. She had been so determined to be miserable, however, that her happiness had become a secret she kept from herself—until her father placed it in her hand like a Brightkey.

"Thanks, Dad," Cordelia said.

She gave him a kiss on the cheek and headed through the open gate. Moments after Mr. Liu pulled away, Cordelia realized that she had left her jacket in the car. She didn't mind. The cold weather didn't bother her anymore.

◆ ◆ ◆

The boy wasn't in his hiding spot, and a block of ice settled in Cordelia's stomach. *Calm down*, she told herself. *That doesn't mean the snatchers got him.* After a few steadying breaths, she forced herself to search the library and quickly found the boy in the fiction section, scanning the shelves like a patron searching for a particular title.

"You scared me," she said.

The boy's mood had slowly been improving over the past few weeks, and he lit up when he saw her. Cordelia smiled in return, but before speaking again checked the library to make sure she was alone. One day she had forgotten and ended up having an awkward conversation with the guidance counselor about how often she talked to herself and whether she thought someone else was really listening.

"It's nice to see you out and about," Cordelia said, bending down.

The boy raised his arms in a fake yawn: *I was bored!*

"Well, good news, then," Cordelia said. "Because I have an exciting job for you. There's a secret room somewhere in this school that has something we need. Trouble is, we don't know where it is. Will you help us find it?"

The boy shook his head and took a few steps toward the safety of his hiding place.

"Please," Cordelia said. "I know it's scary. But I need

you to be brave. If my friends and I find what we're looking for, we might be able to stop the ghost snatchers forever. You wouldn't have to be scared anymore."

The boy raised his eyebrows: *Really?*

"Yes. But if you don't help us, we won't have any chance at all. You understand? We're counting on you."

The boy straightened his glasses and raised his head with newfound determination. He nodded.

"My hero," Cordelia said. "Come with me. There's a photograph I have to show you."

The boy didn't have any luck locating Elijah Shadow's office that week. He must have kept searching over the weekend, however, because when Cordelia returned on Monday, he was waiting for her at the front entrance of the school with a huge grin on his face.

"You found it, didn't you?" she asked.

He nodded, looking very impressed with himself. A few hours later, Cordelia, Benji, and Agnes snuck away during lunch and met the boy outside the library. Since Elijah had wanted his office to remain hidden, Cordelia had assumed the boy would lead them to some dark corner of the school. Instead, they went down to the basement and stopped in the middle of a perfectly ordinary hallway. Cordelia loved it down here. There were two different art rooms located directly across from each other, which meant the air always smelled of creation: clay and paint and freshly sharpened pencils.

Fortunately, the art rooms were empty now.

"Are you sure this is the right place?" Benji asked.

The boy gave him a dark look.

"Just asking," Benji said. "Relax."

Cordelia had noticed that the boy was often cross with Benji for no reason at all. *He's jealous*, she thought. *I'm his only friend in the world, and yet it's Benji who gets to talk to me and see me outside of the school. It must seem so unfair.*

"So where's this office?" Benji asked.

The boy pointed down. Cordelia did the same thing. She had promised Agnes that she would mimic all the boy's movements, like a translator. After everything that had happened, she never wanted Agnes to feel left out again.

"Underground?" Benji asked. Someone had been working on props for the spring play, and the hallway was lined with half-painted wooden trees and Styrofoam boulders. Benji moved one out of the way and checked the hardwood floor beneath it. "Should we be looking for a trapdoor?"

The boy shrugged. Then he started to jump up and down. He seemed intent on making each landing as heavy as possible, as though trying to flatten a box. The fact that he made no sound gave the entire spectacle an eerie, dreamlike quality.

"What's he doing?" Agnes asked, following her friends' eyes to the general location of the boy.

"He's jumping," Cordelia and Benji said in unison.

"Is that some kind of ghost thing?"

"Not usually," replied Benji.

The boy held up a finger—*Give me a second*—then bent his knees and jumped as high as he could, throwing his arms into the air. Instead of landing on the floor, he passed right through it and vanished.

Cordelia told Agnes what had happened.

"That actually makes sense!" Agnes exclaimed. "From what you've told me, ghosts pass through walls like they're not even there. But if that were true for floors, how would they get anywhere? They'd fall through with every step. So ghosts *can* pass through floors, but they really have to work at it."

"Cool," Benji said, searching the spot where the boy had disappeared. "But that doesn't really help us. We can't pass through floors no matter how high we jump."

"That's why the boy shrugged when you asked him if there was a trapdoor," Cordelia said. "He has no idea. All he can do is show us where to go. It's up to us to figure out how to get there."

Cordelia got down on her knees and searched the spot where the boy had passed through the floor, but the only gaps she found were the ones between the hardwood planks. Meanwhile, Benji and Agnes ran their hands along the walls, hoping for some kind of secret lever like the one in the furnace room. The lunch period changed over to recess. Every so often a student would wander down the hall, and the three friends would stop what they were doing and pretend to be having a casual conversation. Cordelia didn't think they were very convincing.

She was about to recommend they give up for now and come back later when Agnes let out a startled gasp.

"I found something!" she exclaimed. Cordelia and Benji joined her, and together they stared at the fabric wallpaper, an elaborate pattern of wildflowers over a black background. Agnes pointed to a light blue hibiscus lost among its more colorful peers.

"Look," she said. "A petal's missing on this flower. When you press that spot the wall feels weird."

Cordelia felt it for herself. The wall was softer in the place the petal should have been, with a slightly gummy feeling.

"Do you think there's a button under there?" she asked.

"If so, it's not doing anything," Benji said, jabbing the spot with his index finger. "How long has it been since someone went down there? If there was a secret door, maybe it doesn't work anymore."

"Or maybe Elijah wanted to make sure no one set it off by accident," Agnes said, "so he made two buttons that had to be pressed simultaneously." She backed away, examining a wider section of the wall. "They would have to be close enough to each other that he could reach them both on his own." She smiled and pointed at the wall. "There! That hibiscus is missing a petal too!"

Cordelia moved aside.

"You do the honors," she said.

Agnes pressed on both hibiscuses at the same time. There was a soft grinding noise, and then a section of the floor rose on iron rods before splitting along the cracks between the planks, creating a passageway.

"We should hurry before someone comes along," Cordelia said, ushering them forward. She peeked into the hole and saw five steps and a lever set into the wall. After that, all was darkness.

"Are we sure this is a good idea?" Benji asked.

224

There was no time to discuss it; they heard footsteps approaching in the distance. The three children scrambled down the steps. Agnes pulled the lever on their way down, and the floor slid back into place, cutting off all light from the world above them.

22

The Guardian

They stumbled around in darkness until Benji finally flicked a light switch. The ancient chandelier above them hissed to life. It glowed brightly for a moment, but then there was a series of loud popping noises as one bulb after another burned out from the unexpected rush of electricity. In the end, only a single bulb remained, spreading a dim, reddish glow throughout the room.

"We actually found it," Benji said, chuckling.

It was definitely the office from the photograph, though it had seen better days. Green patches of mold covered the walls, and the stagnant air was rank with decay. The tall bookcases had splintered and collapsed, spilling their contents onto the floor. A thick layer of dust covered Elijah's drafting table, but other than that it seemed remarkably undamaged. A few drawing tools lay on its surface, including a ruler and an antique bronze compass.

The boy was sitting on top of the cabinets, kicking his legs back and forth. He gave them a cheerful wave.

"We couldn't have found this place without you," Cordelia said.

"Seriously, kid," Benji added. "You rule."

The boy grinned but made a hurry-up motion with his hands.

"The boy thinks we should get a move on," Benji told Agnes. "I happen to agree. I don't like the vibe here."

Cordelia knew what he meant. It was more than just the creepy appearance; the air itself felt heavy. She thought a vocabulary word that she had recently learned in Mrs. Aickman's class described the aura of the room perfectly: *oppressive*.

Cordelia opened a cabinet drawer, releasing a musty smell that made her nose tingle. Inside was a stack of thin, oversized papers a little larger than poster boards. The one at the top was a carefully labeled floor plan for a two-story house. Most rooms hadn't changed much since then—*KITCHEN*, *BEDROOM*, etc.—but there were also a few that Cordelia had never heard of, such as the *ANTECHAMBER*. The dimensions of each room were recorded in a precise, even hand.

"We were right," Cordelia said. "This is where he kept his blueprints!"

"But how do we find the plans for the ghost box in all this?" Benji asked, looking in dismay at the large number of drawers. "This is going to take forever!"

"He must have organized these blueprints somehow," Cordelia said. She pushed the drawer back into place and blew away a cloud of dust, revealing a card inside a brass label holder. It read: *1900–1902*.

"It's organized by year," Agnes said. "That's helpful."

"If we can figure out when he made the plans for a ghost box," Cordelia said.

"Did that illustration Mr. Derleth showed you have a date?"

"Shoot!" Cordelia pounded her head with her knuckles, trying to remember. "Um . . . 1911? 1912? Something like that. Which obviously means Elijah designed the ghost box before then."

"But after his wife died," Benji said. "He wasn't much interested in ghosts before that. When was he born?"

"It was 1881," said Cordelia. "That date I remember."

"Do you know how old he was when he got married?" Benji asked.

"Not sure. But people got married crazy young back then—and Mr. Derleth mentioned that Elijah's daughter was born around the turn of the century."

"And she was still a baby when his wife died," Benji said. "So that must have been . . ."

"Around 1900," Agnes said. "At the earliest. After that, he started wandering around the country, investigating haunted houses. We don't know how long it took him to figure out how to make a ghost box, but I imagine it wasn't right away." She closed her eyes in thought. "Why don't we start with 1904 and see where that takes us?"

"Exactly what I was thinking," Cordelia said. It wasn't, really; she hadn't been able to keep up with their mental math. But she trusted Agnes.

"You guys get started," Benji said. "I want to take a quick look around. These drawers might only be for house blueprints. Maybe Elijah jotted other plans in a journal or something instead."

"Good idea," Cordelia said. "Let's work fast, though. I don't like this place."

She started with the drawer labeled *1904–1906*, while Agnes began with *1907–1908*. The blueprints were a mix of floor plans and exterior designs. The first few houses looked perfectly normal. As Cordelia got deeper into the pile, however, the blueprints grew stranger and more complex. Instead of just one floor plan for the entire house, she found a separate page for each individual room, filled with a complicated array of lines, circles, and measurements that made no sense to Cordelia at all.

This is when he started to play around with archimancy, she thought.

"Guys," Benji said from the other side of the room. There was a slight tremor to his voice. "I think I've . . . um . . . found something."

"The plans?" Cordelia asked.

"Just come here."

"You go," Agnes said, flipping through blueprints at a rapid pace. "I'll keep looking."

The office was a lot bigger than it looked in the photograph, and in order to reach Benji, Cordelia had to climb over a pile of rotting books. She fought back a scream as she saw a rat with a long tail scurry beneath them. Although she knew it was probably just her imagination, her entire body felt itchy, like bugs were crawling all over her.

As soon as I get home, I'm taking the longest shower of all time.

The feeble light from the chandelier barely touched this corner of the office, casting Benji as a dim shape in the shadows. He was standing next to a cot that Cordelia remembered seeing in the photograph.

On the cot was a skeleton.

The bones were surprisingly white, the flesh having been stripped clean long ago, perhaps by the ancestors of the rat currently making its home beneath the books. Tatters of clothes remained. Cordelia thought they might have been pajamas. It was hard to tell in the dark.

"I don't think Elijah Shadow died in a fire," Benji said. "I think he faked his own death so he could hide in this office. I found shelves and shelves of canned food in a big room back there, enough to last for years. Elijah lived here. I'm sure of it." He pointed to the skeleton. "And then he died here."

"Why?" Cordelia asked.

"You got me. But he definitely wanted everyone to think he was dead for some reason."

Cordelia stared at the skeleton, not sure what she should be feeling. Sadness? Horror? Bewilderment? She tried to imagine what it would be like to live here all alone, knowing that the rest of the world was a short flight of stairs away. *What about his daughter? He loved her! What would make Elijah just leave her behind like that?*

"It doesn't make any sense," Cordelia said. "What was he trying to—"

"I've got it!" Agnes shouted in triumph.

They returned to the other side of the room. Agnes had spread a drawing across the drafting table. It looked like the plans for a large wardrobe, with a detailed list of materials and measurements. The words *Spectral Container* had been scrawled along the bottom of the page.

"That's just a fancy way of saying 'ghost box,'" Benji said. "You found it." He gave Agnes a high five. "MVP. Right there."

Agnes blushed so hard that Cordelia thought her face would explode.

Working from bottom to top, Cordelia carefully rolled the plan up; it was brittle, and she didn't want it to tear. She wished they had a hair tie or scrunchie to keep it in place—her hair was too short, Agnes's too messy—but she would just hold it tight for now. The important thing was getting out of the office as quickly as possible. The idea that they might be in some sort of danger was blaring like a fire alarm in her head. She turned toward the exit, anxious for lights and voices and safety.

Elijah Shadow blocked their path.

He looked older than he did in the photograph, with gaunt cheeks and white hair. His eyes, however, burned with the same fire. Cordelia felt a cold sheen of sweat break out all over her body. She had grown somewhat accustomed to ghosts over the past few months, but it was a far different experience when she recognized the man. Elijah Shadow wasn't just a nameless spirit. She had seen proof that he once lived and breathed.

He shouldn't be here, she thought. *This is wrong.*

"What is it?" Agnes asked, noting her friends' horrified expressions.

"Elijah Shadow is standing at the foot of the stairs," Benji whispered. "I don't think he's going to let us leave."

"But he's just a ghost, isn't he?" Agnes asked. "He can't actually do us any harm."

Elijah raised his arm and pointed to their left, where the bronze compass that had been sitting on the table now hovered in the air, its rusty but still serviceable point extended in their direction. As Cordelia watched, the compass was joined by a utility knife and two pairs of scissors, while a row of sharpened pencils took position to their right.

"He's a poltergeist," Benji said. "Terrific."

Elijah pointed again. This time, it was at the plan in Cordelia's hands. He shook his head slowly. Cordelia, wondering if she understood properly, placed the plan on the drafting table and held her hands in the air.

The compass and its army shifted back a few feet,

though they remained hovering in the air. Elijah stepped to the side, clearing the pathway to the stairs.

"We can go," Benji said. "But the plan needs to stay here."

"No way," Cordelia said. "We *need* it."

"We need our lives more, Cord," Benji said, glancing nervously from side to side. "We'll figure out another way."

She stepped forward.

"Hey, Mr. Shadow," she said. "I think I know why you haunt this place. You're guarding these plans, aren't you? So they can't be used by the wrong sort of people."

He gave a barely perceptible nod.

"I understand," Cordelia said. "Only—we're not bad! We want to use your invention to keep the people at Shadow School safe—living *and* dead. You know about the ghost snatchers, right?"

Elijah's face remained impassive, but she saw the slightest hint of distaste at the corner of his lips.

"We want to trap them, so they can't hurt the ghosts anymore. When we're done, we'll bring your plans back. Promise."

Cordelia retrieved the rolled-up sheet of paper. The moment she did, Elijah went back to blocking their path, and the sharp instruments returned to a more threatening position.

"I don't think he's listening," Agnes said.

"Please," Cordelia said, trying to ignore the scissors only a few inches from her left ear. "I know you were a good man. You didn't mean for any of this to happen."

"Cordelia," Benji said. "Put the plans back."

"That means you must be a good ghost too," Cordelia continued. "Let us help—"

The boy came out of nowhere, plowing shoulder-first into the back of Elijah's legs and knocking him over. Cordelia heard a metallic *plink* as the compass and scissors dropped to the ground. Before Elijah could regain his concentration, she ran past him and pulled the lever. The floor started to open. It wasn't fast, allowing Elijah enough time to get to his knees. The boy tried to knock him over again, but Elijah was ready this time and tossed him to the side. Benji and Agnes squeezed through the opening. Cordelia shared one last look with Elijah—his eyes burning with fury—then dashed up the stairs and into the hallway. The bronze compass flew through the opening and impaled itself in the ceiling, missing her by inches.

"Elijah Shadow isn't very nice," Agnes said.

Benji quickly pressed the missing petals on the wall. The floor slid back into place—but not before the boy popped his head out and stumbled to safety. They waited a moment to see if Elijah would follow him, but apparently the office was his ghost zone. He was trapped down there.

"Thank you," Cordelia told the boy. "You were amazing!"

"Absolutely," Agnes said to a point three feet left of the boy. "I mean, I have no idea what just happened. Or where you are. But I'm alive, so whatever you did was perfect."

"We're not only alive," Cordelia said, raising the paper. "We have the plans!"

Plans

"I wish we could go to Dr. Roqueni now," Cordelia said as they sprinted through the halls. "The quicker we get started on building these ghost boxes, the better. Every minute counts."

"Later," Benji said, running harder. "We're epically late for math. We've already escaped death once today. Let's not risk it again."

They ran into the room. Mrs. Machen greeted them with apocalyptic fury.

"What is the meaning of this?" she asked. "You can't just waltz into my class twenty-two minutes late! Have you forgotten how to tell time? Do I need to dig out some first-grade worksheets and give you a review?

Actually, I rather like that idea. Tonight, for homework, you three—"

"It's not that we lost track of time," Agnes said in a perfectly sweet voice. "It's just that your class is so boring it's honestly painful to come here. That's why it took so long. We had to force ourselves to make each and every step."

A stunned silence rocked the class. Miranda's mouth dropped open and her finger began to twitch, as though she couldn't wait to start texting everyone she knew. Mason looked a little impressed.

When Mrs. Machen spoke, it wasn't with the sound and fury that Cordelia expected.

"Report to the principal's office," she whispered. "Now."

They did as they were told.

Dr. Roqueni's office was elegant and spare, with a few Monet prints that Cordelia really liked and a Gauguin that she didn't. A massive whiteboard stretched across one wall. It was covered with dates and schedules.

Dr. Roqueni stared at them from across her desk. She was wearing more makeup than usual as if she were trying to hide the dark circles under her eyes.

"Why are you tormenting Mrs. Machen?" she asked in an exasperated tone.

"We needed to see you," Cordelia said. "Immediately. We've found something important that may help us stop the ghost snatchers."

"That's impossible," Dr. Roqueni said, checking to make sure her door was firmly closed. "Finding something implies searching. And I specifically forbade you to do anything of the sort."

"Well, we did it anyway," Benji said. "Someone had to."

Dr. Roqueni held Benji's gaze for a moment, then looked away and cleared her throat.

"What did you find?" she asked.

They told her almost everything. The hidden office. Elijah Shadow's remains—and his ghost. The drawers of blueprints. Dr. Roqueni didn't say a word the entire time. By the time they finished, she wore the befuddled, groggy look of someone who has just woken up from major surgery.

"I need some tea," she said.

Dr. Roqueni grabbed her mug and left the room. While they waited for her to return, Cordelia noticed a photo sitting on the desk: a group of people posing at a fancy event. They all wore tuxedos and gowns, including the children, and were so similar in appearance that Cordelia suspected they might be related. At the center of the photograph was a lanky black man with slicked-back hair and a gold earring dangling from one ear. He looked like the spitting image of Elijah Shadow, with all traces of kindness scrubbed away.

Uncle Darius, Cordelia thought.

Dr. Roqueni stood slightly apart from the rest of the group. She was about ten years younger and looked lovely and sad in equal measure.

Cordelia heard approaching footsteps and quickly fell back into her seat. Dr. Roqueni entered with a steaming mug of tea. Mr. Ward was right behind her, looking like a giant in the small office. He glanced at the kids without a smile and took his position in the corner of the room.

"The blueprint, please," Dr. Roqueni said, holding out her hand. She seemed to have regained her lost composure. After a moment's hesitation, Cordelia handed it over. Dr. Roqueni reverently spread the plans across her desk. "That's Elijah's signature in the corner," she said with a shudder. "This is genuine."

"Can you build it?" Benji asked Mr. Ward.

"I can build anything," Mr. Ward said, looking down at the plans. "This will take some doing, though. I've never seen anything so intricate before."

"We'll need three of them," Cordelia said. "Maybe more. Can't expect them all to pile into one box."

"Let's not get ahead of ourselves here," Dr. Roqueni

said, retaking her seat. She rolled up the plans and handed them to Mr. Ward. "Do you three children have any idea what you've discovered? My family thought Elijah's work had been destroyed forever. At last, we'll be able to understand how archimancy truly works." A flicker of doubt crossed Dr. Roqueni's face, as though she wondered if unlocking the secrets of archimancy was truly such a good idea, but she swallowed the thought like a bitter fruit. "And if Elijah really faked his own death, like you claim," Dr. Roqueni continued, "who knows what else he created while he was hiding down there? Think of all the secrets in that office, waiting to be discovered." She smiled and met Cordelia's eyes. "My family has fallen on some hard times the past few years, but this is going to save us. And it's all thanks to you."

Cordelia looked away. Despite everything that had happened, she still admired Dr. Roqueni, and the idea that she had impressed the principal filled her with pride. For this reason, Cordelia knew she would have to resist the temptation to give Dr. Roqueni what she wanted.

"That's great news, Dr. Roqueni," Cordelia said. "Especially for you. Your family will be so ecstatic, they might even let you stop being principal. You can finally have the life you always dreamed of—once you know where the office is."

Dr. Roqueni's smile faltered. "So where exactly is it?" she asked, steepling her fingers. "I can't help but notice that you left that particular detail out of your story."

"We can show you right—" Agnes started, but Cordelia placed a hand on her arm, stopping her.

"Here's the thing," Cordelia said. "I think you want to do the right thing and help us. But I'm not a hundred percent sure. You might be more interested in helping yourself. So we're going to keep the location of Elijah's office to ourselves for now."

Dr. Roqueni bit her lower lip.

"You'll tell me after Mr. Ward builds these ghost boxes?" she asked. "That about the size of it?"

"That's right," Cordelia said, acting tougher than she felt. "We don't really have the time to argue about it."

"Why not?" Dr. Roqueni asked. "The snatchers have settled back to their regular routine now that you've stopped disturbing the ghosts. We can take all the time we want. Unless"—she gave Cordelia an appraising look—"there's a particular ghost you want to save, isn't there? That little boy you're always talking to?"

Cordelia tried to hide her surprise that Dr. Roqueni knew about the boy.

"So what?" she asked.

"So time is of the essence for *you*—not for me. You

tell me where the office is, however, and perhaps I can be convinced to work faster."

"Who cares about the stupid office?" Benji asked. "Don't you want to help the ghosts?"

"Of course I do!" Dr. Roqueni snapped. "But I also have some pride, Mr. Núñez. I may not be the best Shadow in the world, but I'm still a Shadow. And I won't be told what to do in my family's home."

Cordelia considered their next step. If she told Dr. Roqueni the location of the office, she had to trust the principal to do the right thing and help them. *But what if she doesn't?* Cordelia thought. *What do I do then?*

Mr. Ward took a step forward. He sniffled once and met Cordelia's eyes.

"Can this box of yours really trap those monsters?" he asked.

"I think so."

"I'll build it, then," he said. "For Dave."

Dr. Roqueni looked livid at this unexpected betrayal.

"How could you—?" she began.

"Come off it, Aria," Mr. Ward said. "You were going to end up helping them and you know it. I'm just moving things along. Besides, I'm starving. I was on my way to town to grab some grub when you yanked me in here. You want something?"

Dr. Roqueni managed to look indignant for another few seconds, but then the anger faded from her face like a passing storm.

"Chicken salad on wheat," she said. "Lightly toasted."

Mr. Ward nodded. "These kids are crazy, Dr. Roqueni," he said, tapping Agnes playfully on the head with the plans as he left. "I kind of like 'em."

24

Night School

Mr. Ward finished the first ghost box two months later. Cordelia, Benji, and Agnes went down to his workshop to check it out. It looked like something one might use to ship a statue across the ocean, save for a reinforced glass window that was the size and shape of a porthole. Although the box looked simply constructed, Cordelia knew better. She had seen what lay hidden between the wooden panels, a cityscape of intricate carpentry that Mr. Ward likened to the inner workings of a clock.

By the time April came around, Mr. Ward had completed the second box and was well into the third. Agnes insisted they continue to patrol the school and make note of which ghosts had vanished and which remained untouched, just to see if the ghost snatchers were doing anything differently. As far as they could tell, it was business as usual. The snatchers didn't suspect a thing.

For the first time, Cordelia started to grow optimistic about their chances.

Then the ghost snatchers came for the boy again.

She found him the next morning huddled in the corner of the library, staring into space. Cordelia had to squint her eyes in order to see him. He was barely visible, like the faded pencil marks of an erased word.

A few minutes later, Cordelia barged into Dr. Roqueni's office.

"We need to move faster!" she exclaimed, pacing back and forth. "If they come for the boy one more time, he'll be gone forever!"

"Sit down, Cordelia," Dr. Roqueni said. "Do you want—"

"If you offer me a cup of tea I'm going to scream!" Cordelia said. She dug her hands into her hair and scratched at her scalp. "We have two boxes ready to go. What if we use them on Geist and Whistler? That should be good enough to stop them for now."

"We've talked about this," Dr. Roqueni said. "It's

best to capture all three at once. Otherwise we sacrifice the element of surprise."

"Well, we have to do *something*," Cordelia said. She threw her head back in frustration. "If I could figure out what his stupid Brightkey is I could save him right now!"

"And risk the snatchers' wrath? We both know that's a terrible idea."

"Well, I don't have any other ones!"

"I do," Dr. Roqueni said. "Bring the boy down to Mr. Ward's office at lunch. He can help us test out the ghost box and see if it actually works."

"I don't see how that helps him," Cordelia said.

"Once the door is closed and locked," Dr. Roqueni said, "the boy won't be able to get out. On the other hand, the ghost snatchers won't be able to get in. He can sleep there at night, safe and sound."

"Oh," Cordelia said, finally taking her seat. "That's a good idea."

"Thank you," Dr. Roqueni said. She folded her hands together and leaned forward. "Correct me if I'm wrong, but this little boy of yours haunted the gym at first, didn't he?"

Cordelia nodded.

"Yet he hasn't remained trapped like the other ghosts.

He can go anywhere he wants now. Have you ever wondered why?"

"I was curious when it first happened," Cordelia said. "But I guess I sort of got used to it since then." She remembered how the boy had responded when she asked him about it in the boiler room. "He said that I was the reason, which makes no sense at all."

"Actually, it makes perfect sense."

"Huh?"

"You talked to him," Dr. Roqueni said. "You showed him warmth and compassion, and he came to care for you in return. The connection between you grew stronger than the archimancy that held him in place. In short, he started haunting you, not the school. It's not the first time such a thing has happened here."

Cordelia knew that Dr. Roqueni was right. She felt it in her bones.

"If that's the case, can he leave and come home with me?" Cordelia asked, hope rising.

"I'm afraid not," Dr. Roqueni replied. She offered an encouraging smile. "But all we need to do is keep him safe a little while longer. We're almost at the end now."

April turned to May, and the students of Shadow School shed their jackets like cicada husks. Mrs. Aickman held class outside and recited tragic nature poems. Ms. Perez organized an art show with an ice cream party afterward. Mr. Bruce's jerseys sprinted toward the home stretch of *U*s and *V*s.

As the day neared when they would finally execute their plan, the kids tried to figure out a way to get the snatchers inside the boxes. The main problem was that they couldn't touch their foe, so grabbing or pushing them was out of the question. Benji suggested using a ghost as bait and then waiting for the right moment to slam the door shut, trapping both the ghost and snatcher inside. This made sense in theory but raised a host of other issues. How would they get the ghost inside the box? Wasn't it cruel to trap an innocent spirit? How could they anticipate the ghost snatchers' location and know where to place a trap?

Just a few days before Mr. Ward completed the final box, Agnes came up with an idea. They met in Dr. Roqueni's apartment after school to discuss it.

"The snatchers only peel one ghost a day," Agnes said. As she talked, she served them chocolate mint brownies that she had baked for the occasion. "And it's not at random. I charted the ghost vanishings by location and began to see a definite pattern to their movements. Since some people weren't consistent about recording their data"—she shot Benji a pointed look—"I can't make as precise a prediction as I'd like, but I've gotten pretty good at guessing which ghost is going to be their nightly target. At least, I can get it down to three possibilities."

"So we have a one-in-three chance of knowing where the ghost snatchers are going to be?" Dr. Roqueni asked with a dubious expression. "You sure about that?"

"Please," Benji said. "It's Agnes."

"I trust her," Mr. Ward said, brushing some crumbs off his beard. "Anyone who can make brownies this good is clearly a genius."

Agnes flashed him a mischievous grin.

"I added crème de menthe," she said. "That's alcohol!"

"All right," Dr. Roqueni said. "We'll go with Agnes's plan. It's definitely a lot easier than running around the school hoping to come across the ghost snatchers. We can pick one of the three possibilities and bring all the ghost boxes to that location. If we're unlucky the first night, we'll try again. One in three is pretty good odds. We're bound to get it right eventually."

The others nodded in agreement—except for Cordelia.

"That'll take too long," she said. "We should divide and conquer—split into three teams, each with one box. This way one of us is sure to find them."

"It's safer to stay together," Dr. Roqueni said.

"But what if we don't find them the first night? Or the second or third or fourth?"

"Then we'll keep trying until—"

"We're *kids*, Dr. Roqueni. We can't just hang out at the school all night whenever we feel like it. What time do the ghost snatchers usually do their thing, anyway?"

"It varies," admitted Dr. Roqueni. "Sometimes they come out the moment the sun goes down. But it could also be much later than that."

"Exactly," Cordelia said. "If we really want to make sure this is going to work, we need to stake out the school all night. We can probably come up with a cover story once—maybe even twice—but that's about it. Our parents aren't stupid."

"Then Mr. Ward and I will do it ourselves," Dr. Roqueni said.

"Mr. Ward can't even see the ghosts," Agnes said. "No offense."

"None taken," Mr. Ward said. "Though to be fair, in the past I've heard a rattling noise late at night. Aria tells me that's their cart."

Strange that he could hear it at all, Cordelia thought. It brought to mind another oddity—how the flashlight she had thrown at the ghostly cart had clanked off its surface, as opposed to passing through it. Cordelia almost brought this up, then decided it was more important to settle on a plan of attack.

"What do you say, Dr. Roqueni?" Cordelia asked. "One night. That's all we need. We'll tell our parents we're sleeping over at each other's houses."

"That only works in movies," Benji said.

Dr. Roqueni gave Cordelia a sympathetic look.

"I know you're worried about the boy," she said. "But there's no rush anymore. He's safe, remember?"

"It's not just the boy," Cordelia said. "It's all of them. Each day that passes is another ghost that will never know its Bright. We've waited long enough, Dr. Roqueni. We need to help them!"

Dr. Roqueni held Cordelia's gaze for a few moments. Finally, she sighed.

"What do you have in mind?" she asked.

That evening, Cordelia, Agnes, and Benji told their parents about a very exciting field trip: they were going to stay overnight at a science museum in Concord! Their parents thought it was unusual that this was the first time they had ever heard of it, but a long email from Dr. Roqueni quickly put their suspicions to rest. *It's a lot easier to lie to your parents when the principal backs up your story*, Cordelia thought.

When the day of the supposed field trip arrived,

Cordelia kissed her parents goodbye and boarded the school bus carrying a duffel bag packed for an overnight trip. Inside were pajamas and a pillow, which she wouldn't need, and a small object that she had found in her mom's old camping gear, which she definitely would.

At five p.m., when all the students lingering after school had finally left, Cordelia and Agnes retrieved one of the ghost boxes from Mr. Ward's workshop, rolled it onto the old gated elevator, and pushed it down the second-floor hallway. The wheels at the bottom had been well oiled, but the box was still heavy and cumbersome, causing the girls to weave back and forth. After a few mishaps, they managed to maneuver the box through the doorway of room 206. The classroom looked as though it hadn't been used in years. There were no desks or chairs, and the walls were bare except for a few inspirational posters featuring smiling children whose clothes must have been the height of fashion three decades ago. A single sentence was scrawled across the chalkboard: *I'M ALWAYS COLD NOW.* Cordelia tried not to think about who might have written it.

They pushed the ghost box to the center of the room. Cordelia took a moment to wipe the sweat from her brow, then slid the heavy-duty barrel bolt to the left.

The door, which could only be locked from the outside, popped open. The box was empty, with enough standing room for two medium-sized adults.

"It reminds me of one of those trick boxes magicians use to make pretty women disappear," Agnes said.

"Same idea," Cordelia replied. "Only with creepy dead guys."

She waved to the boy, who had been in the room since early that afternoon. He was standing next to a frazzled-looking ghost dressed for a long hike: boots, jeans, waterproof coat, backpack. The dead woman spent most days frantically searching every corner of the room with a desperate, confused expression, but the boy's presence had calmed her somewhat. Cordelia could see his lips moving. Though she couldn't hear the words, she knew he was trying to convince the ghost to help them.

"How's it going?" Cordelia asked the boy.

He gave her two thumbs-ups. Or, at least, Cordelia thought he did. She could barely see him at all.

"Let's get her inside," Cordelia said.

The boy guided the hiker to the ghost box. She hesitated for a moment, perhaps second-guessing her decision, so the boy mouthed a few final words of encouragement and pointed to Cordelia. The hiker looked at her with great hope. *He told her what I did for the other ghosts*, Cordelia thought, feeling more pressure than ever. *Now she's counting on me to do the same thing for her.*

The ghost stepped inside the box and folded her arms across her chest. She looked like a body in a coffin—which wasn't, Cordelia supposed, too far from the truth. "Thank you," Cordelia said, leaving the door open so the hiker remained visible to anyone who could see her. She wouldn't be very effective bait otherwise.

Cordelia got down on one knee and faced the boy.

"Good job," she said. "But now you have to convince the other two ghosts to do the same thing. You know the one with the cowboy hat on the fourth floor?"

The boy nodded.

"Go to him first. Benji and Mr. Ward will be there, too. Dr. Roqueni is on the first floor, with a ghost of a little girl about your age, wearing rain boots. You know the one I'm—?"

The boy nodded brightly, giving Cordelia the impression that he and the girl were old friends. She imagined them playing hide-and-seek together in the darkened hallways.

Cordelia held her hands out, palms up, and the boy placed his own hands just above hers. It was their way of holding hands without touching.

"Once the ghosts are inside those boxes, you find a

place far away from all this and hide," Cordelia said in a firm voice. "No playing hero this time around. I don't want you anywhere near the ghost snatchers when they come."

The boy gave her a military salute and vanished through the wall.

"What now?" Agnes asked.

Cordelia took a seat behind an old file cabinet. It wasn't the best hiding spot in the world, but it would have to do. She was counting on the fact that the ghost snatchers didn't see the living very well.

"We wait," Cordelia said. "If the ghost snatchers come to us first, we text the rest of the gang. Everyone rushes over here with their ghost boxes."

"That'll take a few minutes," Agnes said. She rotated her shoulder in its socket. "Those things are heavy."

"Don't worry," Cordelia said. "The first ghost snatcher—Lenny—is a slowpoke. He takes a while to set up before calling the other ones. We should be okay. Besides, for all we know, we might be the ones rushing to help them. There's only a one-in-three chance that the ghost snatchers will come to us first."

Agnes toyed with the whistle tied around her neck. They all wore one. It was for emergencies only. If any of them blew it, that meant they needed immediate help.

"I'm nervous," Agnes said.

"Me too," replied Cordelia. "These guys are scary."

"Not that. I'm worried that when things start happening, I won't be able to help. Like in Elijah's office."

"You'll do great," Cordelia said. "Like always."

She removed the leather pouch she had found in her mother's old stuff and tossed it nervously from hand to hand. *I hope this does the trick*, she thought, settling against the wall. Before long, the sunlight streaming through the window began to fade. Night was falling fast.

25

Whistling in the Dark

Cordelia and Agnes remained vigilant for the first few hours, fear doing more to keep them alert than caffeine ever could. In time, however, the silence and monotony began to wear on them, and both girls found themselves growing exhausted. Around midnight, Agnes curled up on the floor, just "for a minute or two," and almost immediately fell asleep. In order to avoid the same fate, Cordelia remained in constant motion: rocking back and forth on the balls of her feet, doing jumping jacks, circling her arms. She couldn't sit down. If she had, the temptation to close her eyes would have been too great to resist.

There was a rattling noise in the distance.

At first, Cordelia thought it was just her imagination, a standing dream that would soon dissipate like a mirage. She took a few steps toward the open door and listened carefully. Instead of vanishing, the sound grew louder.

It was the ghost snatchers' cart—and it was coming fast.

Cordelia bent down next to Agnes and shook her shoulder. "They're here," she whispered. "Get up, get up!" Unlike Cordelia—who was a groggy, grumpy riser—Agnes was wide awake the moment she opened her eyes. She brushed away a few strands of hair that had fallen loose during her nap and took stock of the situation.

"I hear something," she said, furrowing her brow. "Like a broken shopping cart. It sounds really far away to me."

"It's not," Cordelia whispered. "I think my hearing is just better than yours when it comes to dead things."

"But why can I hear it at all?" Agnes asked, scratching the back of her neck with a thoughtful expression. "Then again, Mr. Ward said he could hear the cart as well, and he can't see ghosts either, so I suppose there must be something different—"

Just beyond the classroom door, squeaking wheels ground to a halt. Cordelia held a finger to her lips and pointed to Agnes's phone: *Text them.* As Agnes tapped away, turning her body to conceal the glow of the LCD screen, Lenny entered the classroom. He looked no different than the first time Cordelia had seen him: blue coveralls, hanging paunch, clipboard in his hands. He made note of the ghost hiker, checking an item off his list, and then walked around the perimeter of the box, eyeing it with a curious expression. Finally, he seemed to decide that the box, though unusual, was nothing worth worrying about, and started back toward the doorway.

Agnes's phone beeped.

She quickly flicked the sound off, but it was too late. Lenny spun around and stared in their direction, squinting his eyes like a student unable to see the chalkboard. Cordelia grabbed Agnes's arm and mouthed *"Don't move."* Although they were only partially hidden, Lenny seemed unable to pin down their location. It was tempting to back deeper into the shadows, but Cordelia's instincts told her that the ghost would have a better chance of sensing motion, like a T. rex.

At long last, Lenny left the room.

"He's gone," Cordelia whispered. "For now, at least."

Agnes exhaled and held up her phone: *On our way*, read the text from Dr. Roqueni. Cordelia breathed a sigh of relief. All they had to do was make it through the next few minutes, and they would no longer be alone.

She heard three metallic bangs in the hallway. And then, after a slight pause, a fourth one, far louder than the others. Agnes clapped her hands to her ears.

"That's how he calls the rest of them," Cordelia whispered. "He did it last time too. Except he only hit the can three times."

Agnes's face grew pale. She bent forward until her lips were next to Cordelia's ear.

"That last one sounded like a warning to the others," she whispered. "I think he knows we're here."

Lenny re-entered the room and placed one of the black A-frame signs in the doorway. *Caution*, Cordelia imagined the sign reading. *Ghost Snatchers at Work*. The sign, however, wasn't the only thing that Lenny had retrieved from the cart. He held a pair of tinted goggles in his hand—the same kind that Geist had been wearing when he caused all the commotion in the lunchroom. Lenny slipped them over his eyes.

When he turned in Cordelia and Agnes's direction this time, a wolfish grin spread across his face. There was no doubt in Cordelia's mind that he could now see them clearly.

The goggles, she thought, panic rising. *They let ghosts see the living.*

Lenny took a step toward them. Cordelia pulled

Agnes to her feet and inched toward the door. The ghost snatcher stepped to the side, blocking their path.

"What's going on?" Agnes asked, her arm looped through Cordelia's. "Why are you shaking?"

"He's looking right at us," Cordelia said, guiding Agnes toward the back of the room. "He has special goggles now."

"Special *what*?"

She jerked to the left, thinking they could slide past the ghost along the far wall, but Lenny positioned himself in the center of the room, ready to cut them off before they could reach the open door. Until this point, the snatcher's movements had been lethargic—just a bored worker doing his job—but now he looked ready for action. The children's impending deaths were probably a fun break from his regular routine.

Stay calm, Cordelia thought, giving Agnes an encouraging smile. *Help should be here any second now. All we have to do is stall a little while longer.* She paced back and forth along the back wall of the room, and the ghost snatcher mirrored her path like a tiger stalking its prey. *He won't attack us unless we try to escape. He's holding us here until his friends arrive.*

There was a thunderous crash one floor below them, like a heavy appliance toppling over. This was followed, almost immediately, by the shrill, desperate notes of a whistle.

"Dr. Roqueni," Agnes said. "She needs help."

They had agreed to blow the whistle only as a last resort, so it was clear that Dr. Roqueni was in serious danger. *Mr. Ward and Benji might have been heading in our direction*, Cordelia thought. *But now they're going to help her first.* She considered blowing her own whistle, but would that be the right thing to do? What if Dr. Roqueni needed help more than they did? What if they had hurt her?

A hot flash of anger incinerated Cordelia's fear.

We don't need help, she thought. *We can do this on our own.*

"Let's split up," Cordelia told Agnes. "You go left, I'll go right. Hopefully it'll confuse him."

"And if it doesn't?"

Cordelia shrugged.

"He can't catch both of us. Whoever escapes can get help."

Agnes looked ready to argue, but Cordelia didn't give her the opportunity. She started along the right-hand side of the room while Agnes, after a brief hesitation, started toward the left. Lenny looked back and forth between the two girls, unsure what to do. *It's probably been decades since he actually had to think about something,* Cordelia thought. *Plus, he doesn't strike me as someone who had a full tank of smart juice, even when he was alive.*

Lenny took a few steps in Agnes's direction, then changed his mind and charged toward Cordelia. As he passed the ghost box, however, the hiker reached out and wrapped her arms around him. Lenny tried to shake her off, but the hiker dragged him backward with a fierce look of determination. Within a few moments, his entire body was inside the ghost box with her.

"Close the door!" Cordelia shouted to Agnes. She would have done it herself, but she needed her hands free in order to toss the leather pouch into the ghost box, just before Agnes slammed the door shut. Lenny, with the feral strength of an animal caught in a trap, threw himself against the door. The two girls worked together to finally bolt it.

Cordelia peeked through the tiny window. Lenny banged his fists against the glass, causing her to jump back in surprise, but the hiker was nowhere to be seen. Cordelia assumed she had knelt out of sight.

"Is it working?" Agnes asked.

"I'm not sure," Cordelia replied—but then the hiker rose into view, looking carefully at the object Cordelia had thrown into the box: a silver compass. "Yes!"

Cordelia exclaimed, pumping her fist in triumph. "She's holding it! She wouldn't be able to do that if it wasn't her Brightkey!"

A black triangle appeared above the ghost box. It slid open, setting the room aglow with neon light and unleashing an orchestra of city sounds: beeping horns, jackhammers, reggae music blasting from a car radio. The hiker floated out of the box with a beatific smile on her face and ascended into her Bright.

City girl, Cordelia thought, imagining the woman's whole sad story. *Took a weekend trip to the forest and got lost.*

"We trapped the bad ghost," Cordelia told Agnes. "And saved the good one."

She felt a tear run down her cheek. It had been a long time since she'd helped a ghost, and she had missed it.

"Go us," Agnes said. "But there are two more of those things out there. Plus, we have to help Dr. Roqueni."

Cordelia nodded and ran into the hallway. She nearly crashed into Lenny's cart, which was parked just outside the door, but managed to twist to her left and dodge it at the last moment. Agnes wasn't so lucky. She hit the cart at full speed, a glancing blow that sent her spinning. As Agnes fell, the cart tottered on two wheels before gravity set things right again. A few supplies dropped to the floor.

"Ow!" Agnes said, holding her side. "What was *that*?"

"The cart," Cordelia said. "I'm sorry—I should have told you it was there. I guess it's not incorporeal like the ghosts. Just invisible."

"That's why Mr. Ward and I could hear it," Agnes said, wincing in pain as she sat up. Her fingers brushed against a pair of goggles that had been knocked from the cart. "There's something here. I can't see it, but I feel it. Do you know what it is?"

Before Cordelia could reply, something touched her shoulder from behind. She spun around and screamed at the same time.

"Shh!" Benji said, grabbing her wrists. "They're gonna hear us!"

"Why did you sneak up on me?"

"I was trying to be stealthy," Benji said. He noticed Agnes struggling to stand and slid past Cordelia to help her. "You okay?"

"Banged up my knee. But I'll live."

"Good," Benji said. "We need to get out of here. Now."

"Where's Dr. Roqueni and Mr. Ward?" Cordelia asked.

"I'll tell you on the way," Benji said. He started down the hall at a sprint, then realized how much trouble Agnes was having and returned to help her. She could limp along at a steady pace, but running was out of the question. They made their way to the end of the hall. Benji held up a hand and then peeked around the corner before waving them along.

"The ghost snatchers didn't stay together like we thought they would," Benji said. "Geist found Dr. Roqueni. She tried to get him inside the ghost box, but he used his powers to toss it into her. The box was destroyed, and Dr. Roqueni was hurt really bad. She whistled for help."

"We heard," Cordelia said.

"Mr. Ward carried her out of the school," Benji said. "He told me to stay with her while he went back inside to get you guys, but I ran off before he could stop me. It doesn't make sense for him to go. I'm the one who can see the ghosts."

"That was really brave," Cordelia said.

Benji shrugged like it was nothing, but even in the dim light she could see the blush creeping along his neck.

"We're not out of it yet," Benji said as they approached another corner. "We still need to get downstairs. Geist is guarding the main stairs, and the one with the slicked-back hair—"

"Whistler," Cordelia said.

"—he's standing in front of the west stairwell. They

know you're up here. They're just waiting for you to come down."

Cordelia decided that Agnes had been correct about Lenny's fourth strike against the garbage can—it had been a signal that there were intruders in the school. The other two ghost snatchers had immediately done a search and found Dr. Roqueni.

"So where to, then?" Agnes asked. "East stairwell?"

Benji shook his head.

"That'll take us too close to Geist. I have a better idea."

They raced through the school, using every short-cut that Benji and Cordelia had discovered during their months helping the ghosts, until they reached room 235.

"Mr. Blender's room," Agnes said with a smile. "Perfect."

Hundreds of eyes watched them enter. Mr. Blender, a colorful old man who favored vests and musical ties, had an unusual tradition: at the end of each year he painted life-size portraits of his students directly onto the walls. After twenty years of teaching, nearly every inch of white space had been covered, making the room feel like a haunted amphitheater.

"This is one of my favorite rooms during the day," Cordelia said, looking around uneasily. She wasn't sure what kind of paint Mr. Blender had used, but the eyes of his former students seemed to glow in the dark. "Can't say I care for it much at night."

"We're just passing through," Benji said, kneeling down next to the second unique feature of room 235: a trapdoor that led to the library. Mr. Blender had painted a swirling portal on it and the fanciful phrase *GATEWAY TO OTHER WORLDS.*

"Let's climb down fast and make a run for it," Benji said. "Don't use the main entrance—Geist will definitely see us. Head left, toward the door that leads to the parking lot."

"Students aren't allowed to use that door," Agnes said.

Cordelia and Benji stared at her in disbelief.

"Sorry," Agnes said.

"Here we go," said Benji, gripping the handle with both hands.

He lifted the trapdoor, and Cordelia peered down into the darkness. A man wearing dark goggles was standing at the bottom of the ladder. He looked up at her and grinned. Cordelia caught a flash of movement as Benji reached for something in his pocket, then the man below her began to whistle. It was a different tune from the one Cordelia had heard the first time she saw him. The music wrapped itself around her, squeezing the tension from her muscles and soothing all her worries. Cordelia knew she should run, especially when she saw Whistler climb the first few rungs of the ladder, but moving required a huge amount of energy that she no longer possessed.

From the corner of her eye, she saw that Benji and Agnes were frozen as well.

Move, Cordelia! she told herself, watching the ghost snatcher's approach with growing unease. He continued to whistle. It seemed like he could do it all day. Climbing the ladder, on the other hand, was serious work, so Whistler abandoned the rungs and floated skyward like an astronaut in zero gravity. He landed gracefully on the classroom floor and patted down his gelled hair in order to make sure it was perfect. For a moment he was confused—there were kids everywhere, even in the walls!—but then his eyes settled on the three children in front of him. He inspected each one of them from top to bottom, then repeated the process a second time. He began to whistle a different tune. It sounded like something you might hear during the final question of a quiz show—a soundtrack for difficult decisions.

Finally, he stopped before Agnes and waved his hand in front of her face. When she didn't react, he gave Cordelia a big wink and held his hands to Agnes's cheeks.

She instantly began to shiver.

Get off her! Cordelia tried to scream, but she couldn't move her lips. She remembered the times that ghosts had brushed against her in the past, the coldness that numbed her body for hours afterward. *And that had only been a passing touch,* Cordelia thought. *What if they never let go?*

Agnes's lips began to turn blue.

We don't have much time, Cordelia thought, her racing heart pounding against its useless cage. She shifted her eyes to the left and saw that Benji had somehow managed to lift his hand all the way to his mouth. Cordelia was glad to see him defy the ghost snatcher, but she didn't see how touching his mouth could possibly help.

Then she saw the whistle in his hand.

Benji blew it. The shrill sound was deafening in the small room, overpowering Whistler's song. Cordelia felt her power of movement return. She quickly grabbed Agnes, who was freezing cold to the touch, and helped her out of the room. Once she was safe, Cordelia returned to help Benji—just in time to see Whistler snatch the whistle from his mouth. The ghost reached out his other hand, no doubt planning to freeze Benji just as he had tried to do with Agnes—and then suddenly paused with a confused expression on his face.

He looked down at the whistle.

He doesn't understand how he could possibly be holding it, Cordelia thought. *Come to think about it, neither do I. His hand should have passed right through it.* A shocking thought occurred to her. *Unless . . .*

The ghost snatcher's befuddled expression turned to one of ardent fascination. He raised the whistle closer to his eyes so he could drink in every detail. Cordelia used this opportunity to take Benji's hand and lead him away. Whistler didn't notice. For the time being, nothing else existed except the tiny piece of musical metal sitting in his hand.

A red triangle appeared.

Instead of hovering in the air like its black siblings, the triangle lay flat on the floor, gleaming like a poisonous candy apple. It slid open. Puffs of smoky darkness polluted the room. From deep within the bowels of the triangle, Cordelia heard factory sounds: the pump of pistons, rumble of heavy machinery, roar of a furnace.

And screams. There were lots of screams.

Whistler tossed away the Brightkey—*or Darkkey,* Cordelia thought—and tried to escape. The triangle slid along the floor, hunting him like a shark. The ghost snatcher made it to the other side of the room before taking a step into nothingness and falling through the portal.

The triangle slammed shut and vanished.

Agnes, still shivering, re-entered the room. Without a word, they took the ladder down to the library. No one wanted to discuss what they had just witnessed. There was one detail that Cordelia still didn't understand, however.

"How were you able to blow the whistle?" she asked Benji. "I couldn't move at all."

"What?" he asked, not hearing her. "Oh!" He slipped off his earbuds. "I put these on the moment we saw Whistler. I wasn't sure if he'd be able to affect the living like he did the ghosts, but better safe than sorry."

"Smart thinking," Agnes said, blowing on her hands. "Now can we please get out of here? I want to lie underneath fifty blankets next to a roaring fireplace."

Their trip to the side door was surprisingly uneventful. Agnes went first into the warm May night, followed by Benji. Cordelia had just taken her first step across the threshold when she sensed a change in the air. She paused with her hand on the door and glanced over her shoulder. The boy was hovering at the end of the hallway. He kicked and waved his hands like a bad swimmer, trying to escape the invisible claws that held him in place.

Geist, Cordelia thought. *He's using his powers on the boy. It's a trap, obviously. Geist knows if I leave the school he won't be able to hurt me anymore. So he's giving me a reason to stay.*

The boy began to drift away, floating like a balloon into the deeper darkness at the end of the hall. In a few moments, Cordelia could no longer see him at all. Panic welled up in her chest.

I can't just abandon him! she thought. *What choice do I have?*

"You okay, Cord?" Benji asked from the parking lot. "Why are you just standing there?"

Cordelia pulled the door shut. It locked automatically. There was no way for Benji and Agnes to get back inside the school without a key.

Her friends ran to the door and pounded on the glass.

"Have you lost your mind?" asked Agnes. "Get out of there!"

"Geist has the boy," Cordelia said. "I have to help him."

"Listen to me, Cordelia," Benji said, placing his palms flat against the glass door. "You can't fight him. He'll kill you."

"Just like he killed David Fisher," added Agnes. "I

know the boy's important to you, but you have to let him go."

Cordelia shook her head.

"I can't do that," she said, and raced down the hallway until the darkness of Shadow School swallowed her whole.

Geist

Cordelia sped around the corner, hoping to find the boy. Instead, she found a ghost box. It was about thirty feet off, sitting in the precise center of a long, locker-lined hallway. Cordelia was thrilled by this sudden stroke of good luck. After all, there was only one ghost box left, and she was going to need it to stop Geist. It was amazingly fortunate that Benji and Mr. Ward had left it here.

Except I just came down this hallway three minutes ago, Cordelia realized, the smile fading from her face. *And that box was definitely not here.*

She took a few hesitant steps down the hall. *Why would Geist leave the box for me?* she wondered. The door was closed, the lock bolted shut. Cordelia caught a flash of movement behind the window. *Is there something terrible inside? Some kind of new horror that he left just for me?*

A few steps later, she saw that it was the boy.

He met her eyes and frantically shook his head: *Don't come any closer!* Cordelia figured the boy was trying to protect her, but she continued to approach the box anyway, looking warily from side to side. She didn't see Geist anywhere.

He must be looking for Whistler and Lenny, Cordelia thought. *Geist probably didn't expect me to return so soon. If I hurry, I might be able to free the boy before he comes back.*

The lockers to either side of her began to rumble and shake.

"Uh-oh," Cordelia said.

Locks burst open and shot across the hall at dangerous speeds. Cordelia heard one whiz past her ear while another clipped her wrist, sending a lightning bolt of pain all the way to her elbow. She broke into a run. The ghost box was only ten feet away, and once she freed the boy, she thought she could use it as shelter until Geist's attack passed. Before she could reach the box, however, the locker doors flew open and unleashed a tornado of school supplies. Within moments, Cordelia was bombarded by dry-erase boards, notebooks, pencils, calculators, and textbooks. She fought her way against the storm until a dictionary-thick volume smacked her right temple with a sickening thud. Cordelia collapsed, and the offending book landed right in front of her: *Algebra II: A Real-World Approach.*

I hate math, Cordelia thought.

The world went dark.

When Cordelia opened her eyes, she felt like she was moving. At first, she assumed this was just dizziness, but then she realized that she was inside the ghost box. Someone was pushing it.

The boy was inside the box as well, watching her with a look of concern.

"I'm okay," Cordelia said. "It's just a bump."

She tried to stand, but the world began spinning like a carousel. Cordelia decided to remain seated on the floor of the box until her equilibrium returned.

"Any idea where he's taking us?" she asked.

The boy shook his head.

Cordelia assumed that knocking her out and putting her in the ghost box had been Geist's plan all along. *Is this his revenge for what I did to Lenny?* she wondered. *Does he want me to see what it feels like?* Cordelia wasn't completely sold on this theory; Geist didn't seem the type to seek revenge for his fallen allies. If anything, he probably wanted to punish her for using the ghost boxes in the first place. *Maybe he's taking us to some hidden room in the school, where I'll be trapped inside the box forever, even after I turn into a ghost.*

They stopped moving.

Cordelia heard the bolt lock disengage. She cautiously pushed the door open and stepped out of the box. She was back in the hallway outside room 206. Geist was standing in front of the cart. He wasn't wearing his tinted goggles. Whatever happened next, he wanted to see it with his own eyes.

The boy started to follow her out of the box, but Geist flicked his wrist and the door slammed shut, locking him inside. Cordelia suddenly rose two feet into the air and drifted toward the cart. She tried to fight it, but Geist was too powerful. He didn't stop moving her until she was hovering over the garbage can.

Geist removed the lid.

Cordelia found herself looking down a white chute that extended far beyond the physical limits of the can. She couldn't even see the end of it. *So that's what happened to David Fisher,* Cordelia thought, fear building in the pit of her stomach. She felt guilty that her parents would never know what happened to her.

Cordelia fell.

Instead of plummeting headfirst down the chute, as Geist no doubt intended, she landed half in and half out of the can, folded over at her hips. She tried to stand, but her feet didn't reach the floor, and rocking backward only made her slide farther. *Stay calm*, she told herself, reaching out her hands to try to gain some purchase on the wall of the chute itself. It was slick to the touch and warmer than she thought it'd be. For a moment, it seemed to undulate beneath her fingers.

Is this thing alive? Cordelia wondered.

Her hands slipped on the wall, and she slid forward six inches. Momentum carried her deeper and deeper into the chute. In just a few moments, she would be past the point of no return and free-falling into its impossible depths. Before that happened, however, hands grabbed her ankles and pulled upward, lifting her out of the chute and back into Shadow School. She and her rescuer fell onto the floor in a tangle of arms and legs.

"Thanks," Cordelia said to Benji. "I thought I was—"

"Later," Benji said. "Agnes needs our help."

Cordelia got to her feet and tried to catch up on all she had missed. Agnes, wearing the tinted glasses that had fallen from the cart, had dug one of the snatching tools into Geist's back. The ghost kept trying to escape her grasp, but Agnes was able to follow each one of his movements and shift her weight accordingly.

That's because she can see him, Cordelia thought. *Those*

goggles don't only help ghosts see the living. They help the living see ghosts!

Even with Agnes's newfound ability, Geist was proving difficult to capture. He was on the verge of slipping away altogether when Benji clamped a second snatching tool to his left leg and pulled backward.

"Cordelia!" Agnes exclaimed, beads of sweat running down her face. "Help us!"

Cordelia grabbed a tool of her own and got to work, fastening the claw to Geist's hip. The ghost snatcher spun in her direction, his green eyes glowing with malevolence, but there was nothing he could do: the three friends had triangulated their attack, and he was trapped within it.

"Pull!" Benji exclaimed.

Cordelia set her feet like a tug-of-war player during a championship game and pulled with all her strength. For a few moments, she seemed to make no progress whatsoever, then something within Geist snapped apart, and all three kids fell backward. When Cordelia sat up, she noticed two things. One, Geist was gone. Two, each one of their snatching tools now held a sad, deflated sac of skin.

They threw them in the garbage can.

27

Endings and Beginnings

Cordelia was nervous that Elijah Shadow might jump out and attack her as soon as she re-entered his office, but it turned out that he wasn't the kind of ghost to hold a grudge. *Besides, I'm not stealing something this time*, she thought. *I'm putting it back.*

Cordelia slid open the appropriate drawer and returned the plans for the ghost box.

"It's hard to convey what a big deal this is for my family," Dr. Roqueni said. It was her first time inside the office, and she looked close to tears. "It's like our own personal holy grail."

"What did they say when you told them?" Cordelia asked.

Dr. Roqueni scratched beneath the cast on her wrist.

"I called Uncle Darius last week to let him know that the ghost snatchers were no longer an issue at Shadow School. He was very impressed. He gave me his blessing if I wanted to return to Paris. In fact, he told me he could pull some strings and get me a curating job at the Louvre—my lifelong dream."

"Congratulations," Cordelia said, forcing a smile. "I'm really happy for you."

"I told him no," Dr. Roqueni said. "I have found, quite to my surprise, that I actually enjoy being the principal of Shadow School. For some reason, I needed the option to leave before I understood that." Dr. Roqueni crossed the room and stood over Elijah's bones. She bowed her head reverently. "Good morning, Great-Great-Grandfather. I'm sorry you've been down here in the dark for such a long time."

"Should we bury him?" Cordelia asked.

"No," Dr. Roqueni said, looking past Cordelia. "I think he's right where he wants to be." Cordelia spun around and saw Elijah's ghost nodding with approval. "However," Dr. Roqueni continued, clapping her hands together, "we can certainly make his stay a good deal more pleasant." She pointed to the old chandelier, which barely lit the room. "The first thing we're going to do is replace that thing with something that actually works. Then we're going to sort through those books and see what we can salvage."

"We?" Cordelia asked.

"Well, I can't do it on my own," she said. "I'm not ready to tell my family about this place. Not until I know what secrets it contains. If Elijah went to such an extent to keep this office hidden, he might have done so for a very good reason. We need to catalog and organize everything."

"Catalog?" Cordelia asked. "Organize? Agnes is going to be in heaven. Not so sure about Benji."

"There is one other thing," Dr. Roqueni said. "I don't think Uncle Darius believed everything I told him over the phone. He's planning a visit in the fall. And when he comes, you and Benji need to hide your gifts at all costs."

"Why?" Cordelia asked.

Dr. Roqueni looked at her with concern.

"Because if you don't, I'm afraid he'll make use of you."

A few days later, Mr. Derleth asked Cordelia to drop by after school. She figured he wanted to talk about her grades. They hadn't been very good since the business with the ghost boxes began, and she hoped she had enough time to improve them before the year ended.

"Good afternoon, Cordelia," he said when she entered. "Take a seat."

Mr. Derleth looked even sadder than usual today. His eyes were red-rimmed and puffy, as though he had been crying right before she entered. She saw a box of tissues on his usually barren desk.

"Everything okay?" she asked.

"Right as rain," he said. Mr. Derleth cleared his throat and rose from his chair. "There're just a few things I want to ask you. It would be best if you were honest with me, though. I'm a little tired of being lied to."

He walked over to the door and closed it. Then, after the slightest hesitation, he locked it as well.

"What's going on?" Cordelia asked.

"You tell me," Mr. Derleth said, pulling down the shade so no one could see inside the room. There was an uncharacteristic edge to his voice. "You seem to know everything that goes on in this place."

"I'd like to leave now, Mr. Derleth," Cordelia said. "You're scaring me."

"Well, that makes two of us, Cordelia," he said. "I'm scaring me too. But you're not leaving this room until I know one thing. I've done the research. I've talked to Dr. Roqueni and the other teachers here. I've searched the school, time and time again. It's gotten me nowhere. So that leaves you, Cordelia. My last hope."

"What are you talking about?"

"A few months ago, you sat in that very chair and told me there were no ghosts in Shadow School. That Elijah Shadow was—your word—'bonkers.' In light of recent events, I believe that you were lying. So I'm going to ask you again. And I beg you: please tell me the truth this time, for both our sakes. Is Shadow School haunted?"

It was the sadness in his eyes, more than the anger, that made Cordelia tell the truth. "Yes," she said.

Mr. Derleth gasped.

"Thank you, Cordelia," he said, visibly shaken. "Thank you for at last being honest with me. Now another question, even more important than the first. Who haunts Shadow School?"

"It's not just one person," Cordelia said. "There're too many to count."

Mr. Derleth seemed surprised by this response. He reached into his desk drawer and pulled out a framed photo.

"How about him?" Mr. Derleth asked. "Does he haunt Shadow School?"

This time it was Cordelia's turn to gasp.

The photograph was of the boy.

◆ ◆ ◆

286

Cordelia stared out the window of her room. She could see the peaks of the White Mountains in the distance. Next year, she wanted to go skiing.

She thought about what she had learned.

The boy's real name was Owen Tyler Derleth. He'd died two years ago. Cordelia didn't know how. Mr. Derleth skipped over that part of the story, and Cordelia didn't ask. After his son's death, Mr. Derleth had a hard time. He stopped going to work and lost his job. Mrs. Derleth left. On the advice of a friend, he went to a psychic. Mr. Derleth hoped to receive some comforting news about his son being at rest so he could move on with his own life. Instead, the psychic told him that Owen's spirit was trapped and needed to be rescued. She even told him where. At first, he didn't believe her, but the more that Mr. Derleth researched the school, the more he feared that there might be something to it. Fortunately, there were always jobs available at Shadow School, which allowed Mr. Derleth to secretly conduct his investigation.

Cordelia had shown him her drawing of the boy, and Mr. Derleth had sobbed for a long time. Afterward, Cordelia had explained about Brightkeys, and how the boy's appearance should provide them with the clues they needed to set him free. Mr. Derleth identified the boy's Brightkey immediately. Cordelia didn't feel bad about not being able to figure it out herself. It was something only his father would know.

Now there's just one thing left to do, Cordelia thought.

She walked into the living room. Her parents were on the couch, watching a young couple on HGTV decide if an old Victorian was worth the price.

"Hey," Cordelia said. "Can I sit with you guys for a while?"

"Always," Mrs. Liu said, holding out her arms.

Cordelia snuggled between her parents. It was like old times. It was also something new.

They gathered in the gym after school. This was where it had all begun, so Cordelia thought it should end there as well. Agnes was still limping a little after her collision with the ghost cart, but according to the doctor she would be walking just fine by summer. Benji was wearing his soccer uniform. He had rejoined the team that week—much to the delight of Mr. Bruce—and had his first game later that afternoon. Cordelia and Agnes were going to watch him play, and then all three of them were planning to head into town for ice cream.

Mr. Derleth was there as well. He had dressed up for the occasion in a suit and tie. He held a small jewelry box in his hands.

"Are you sure you don't want these?" Agnes asked, holding out a slim black case. Inside were the goggles that would allow even those without the Sight to see ghosts.

"I'm tempted," Mr. Derleth said. "But I think I'd rather remember Owen the way he was, full of life and joy." He scanned the gym. "Is he here?"

Owen was standing right next to Cordelia. He squinted up at Mr. Derleth without a hint of recognition. Cordelia wasn't surprised. The boy hadn't recognized his name when she told it to him, either. Agnes called it "spectral amnesia."

"He's so happy to see you," Cordelia told Mr. Derleth. "You should see the smile on his face!"

Owen gave her a strange look.

"What do I do?" Mr. Derleth asked.

"Just open the box and put it on the floor," Benji said. "That's all there is to it."

Mr. Derleth followed Benji's directions. Inside the box was a single stamp of a green-and-blue locomotive. It said *JERSEY* at the top and was worth three pence. A postmark had marred the stamp with straight black lines.

"Look, Owen," he said. "Your favorite stamp. Just like the one on your shirt."

The boy looked down at his pajamas. He saw the

match and smiled in wonder.

"Do you remember how you used to curl up in bed next to me and we would look through my collection together?" Mr. Derleth asked. "The train stamps were always your favorites."

Owen picked up the stamp. Unlike the other potential Brightkeys that Cordelia had tried over the past months, he had no problem holding it. Mr. Derleth's mouth fell open as the stamp floated before his eyes.

"Is that Owen doing that?" he asked. "Is that my boy?"

"Yes, Mr. Derleth," Benji said. "It's working. He'll be at peace soon."

A black triangle appeared above the boy. It slid open. Sunlight filled the gym. Cordelia could hear children playing and the squeaking sound of a swing going back and forth. The boy began to the rise into the air.

Instead of welcoming his Bright, however, he looked back at Cordelia and held out his arms.

No, he mouthed, shaking his head. *Stay!*

The boy stopped rising.

"He's fighting it," Benji whispered, placing a hand on Cordelia's shoulder. "You have to stop him. I don't think you get another chance at this kind of thing."

The boy dropped to the ground. Above him, the black triangle began to slide shut.

"I know you're scared," Cordelia said, tears obscuring her vision. "But it's going to be wonderful. Listen! Do you hear that?"

From within the boy's Bright came the *chugga-chugga-chugga* of an approaching train. A whistle blew. The boy listened with interest. The black triangle stopped closing and began to open again.

"It'll be here soon," Cordelia said. "You don't want to miss it. Who knows where it will take you?"

The boy drifted upward. This time, he didn't fight it. He gave Cordelia a wave, as though he was just going on a fun trip and would be back again soon, and she waved back. At the last moment, he looked down at Mr. Derleth, and Cordelia saw sudden recognition illuminate his eyes. *Hey, Daddy!* he mouthed. It wasn't with sadness. The boy didn't know sadness anymore. He ascended into the Bright, but just before the triangle closed Cordelia heard his voice for the first time.

He said her name—and goodbye.

RETURN TO SHADOW SCHOOL:

Read on for a sneak peek at the next book!

Ghost Race

A man stood in the corner of Ms. Dalton's social studies classroom. He looked slightly confused, like a visiting parent who had gotten lost. If you didn't know any better, you would have thought he was alive.

Cordelia Liu knew better.

She stepped closer, examining every inch of the ghost. Her gaze was steady, her breathing unhurried. Any other twelve-year-old would have run screaming, but Cordelia knew much of the lingering dead and found nothing here to frighten her. She calmly noted the tags from a dozen ski slopes dangling from the man's winter coat, the chapped skin of his windburned cheeks, his woolen hat. After learning what she could from the man's appearance, Cordelia slid into a chair in order to observe his actions. The ghost paid her no heed, focusing instead on a point far in the distance, perhaps seeing a world invisible to living eyes. After a few moments, he squinted and raised one gloved hand to his forehead, as though fighting the glare of the sun. Since the curtained windows permitted only a trickle of light into the room, Cordelia knew that the ghost wasn't actually having trouble seeing. He was trying to tell her something.

"Ski goggles," Cordelia said.

She slung her backpack off her shoulders and began rifling through its contents. The only way to free a ghost trapped within the walls of Shadow School was by delivering its Brightkey, which was an object that had been of special significance to the deceased. Since ghosts couldn't talk, Cordelia had to rely on the clues provided by their appearance and actions. Often these clues were difficult to decipher, but sometimes, as with the man before her, the answer was obvious.

"Goggles, goggles," she muttered, digging past the other potential Brightkeys she had grabbed from their new storage room: colorful silk scarves, a battered copy of *David Copperfield*, three double-A batteries. "I know they're here somewhere . . ."

She paused to flick the sweat from her brow. Usually

the interior of Shadow School was as cool as a crypt, but the temperature had been hovering in the low nineties all week—a virtual heat wave for New Hampshire—and Cordelia's tank top was soaked with sweat. The ghost, of course, didn't seem to notice the heat at all.

"Yes!" Cordelia exclaimed, spotting the ski goggles at the bottom of her bag. She yanked them out and checked the time on her phone: 11:58. *Two minutes to go,* she thought. The ghost stared at the goggles dangling from her hand, confused, then bent his knees and swiveled his hips from side to side.

"You like to ski," Cordelia said. "I'm on it. Promise. I'd give you these goggles right now, but I'm having this race with my friends to see who can rescue the most ghosts in an hour, and we're not supposed to start until noon on the dot. Kinda silly, I know, but it was the only way to get my friend Benji to come help. He's been sitting in his house playing video games since the beginning of summer."

Her phone dinged. "Here's Lazybones now," Cordelia said. Benji Núñez had sent her a text:

You ready to go down, Liu?

Please, Cordelia texted back. *Unlike u I have a plan*

I don't need a plan. I have SKILLZ.

Maybe at soccer but I'm the GHOST MASTER.

We'll see about that. I'm sending 8 spooks home. At least.

3

In an hour???? Nope

Watch me

U won't top 5

Still be more than you!

A tiny photo of a platypus wearing a lab coat appeared as Agnes Matheson, the third member of their group, joined the chat.

It's adorable the way you two are fighting over second place. You both know I'm going to win, right?

Check out Ag with the trash talk! replied Benji. *We've taught her well.*

So proud, added Cordelia.

I'm just happy that I can finally see them, replied Agnes, which prompted a flurry of smiley-face emojis from both her friends. The students and teachers of Shadow School were oblivious to the spirits that roamed its halls; to the best of Cordelia's knowledge, only she, Benji, and Dr. Roqueni, the school's principal, had the natural ability to see them. This had initially created some tension with Agnes, who'd felt like an outsider since the spirits remained invisible to her. Fortunately, she had discovered a special pair of goggles that allowed her to see them, and now the three friends were on equal footing. Cordelia suspected that helping the ghosts would be much easier from now on—and a lot more fun.

The clock on her phone changed to 12:00.

GAME TIME!!!!!!!!!!!!!!!!!!!!!!!! Benji texted.

Cordelia didn't reply. Instead, she slid the ski goggles across the floor, expecting the ghost to eagerly snatch them up.

He ignored them.

"Come on, Casper," Cordelia muttered, zipping up her backpack and slinging it over her shoulder. "I haven't got all day."

She couldn't leave without visual confirmation that the ghost had been freed—otherwise it wouldn't count toward her score. The clock was ticking, however, and she wanted to make sure she snagged some of the easier ghosts before Benji or Agnes got to them first.

Her phone dinged.

One down! Benji texted. *The woman staring at that creepy glass carousel. Ticket to an amusement park.* This text was followed almost immediately by one from Agnes: *Wet guy! Umbrella!*

"You're killing me here!" Cordelia told the skier. Then, realizing what she had said, added, "Sorry."

At last, the ghost's eyes settled on the goggles. Cordelia felt her shoulders tense as he leaned forward to pick them up. If they weren't his Brightkey, his hand would pass right through them.

The moment of truth, she thought, biting her lower lip.

The ghost lifted the goggles with ease.

"Boom!" Cordelia exclaimed.

Above the skier, a black triangle appeared. As the entrance to the portal slid open, swirling snow-flakes descended from the man's Bright, vanishing the moment they touched the floor. From the world beyond the triangle, Cordelia heard the swish of skiers speeding down a slope, the grinding gears of a lift, laughter. The ghost smiled with delight and rose toward the portal. He pulled the goggles on—they were a little loose, but Cordelia had learned that such details usually didn't matter—and raised his hands into the air, eager for the ski poles that would no doubt be awaiting him on the other side. Cordelia forgot about the hurry she was in and watched in fascination. The sight of a ghost being freed from Shadow School and transported to its own personal paradise never failed to fill her with awe.

Her phone dinged again. Benji.

Jogger. Shoelaces. THAT'S TWO!

Cordelia grunted. The jogger, a new arrival who spent her days stretching outside Mr. Terpin's math class, had been her next stop. Cordelia had been plan-ning to try a pair of earbuds first, but she had also brought shoelaces just in case. A mystifying number of ghosts wanted to spend their afterlife jogging, and it was inevitably one or the other.

Skier, Cordelia texted, already moving. *Goggles. Just*

getting warmed up.

She broke into a run, navigating the labyrinthine halls of Shadow School with practiced ease. Cordelia would be okay if Agnes beat her—well, sort of okay—but not if Benji did. *I'll never hear the end of it*, she thought, sprinting past boxes of classroom supplies waiting to be unpacked and silent, summer-clean classrooms: chairs stacked, chalkboards scrubbed, sharpeners emptied. The school, for all intents and purposes, was in a state of hibernation until the students returned in six weeks.

Asleep, Cordelia thought, but not empty. Shadow School is never empty.

After her slow start with the skier, Cordelia found her rhythm and freed three more ghosts: a girl with a cool punk vibe chilling in room 222 (spiked leather bracelet); a businessman who looked inconvenienced by his demise, as though missing out on a few big deals were the worst of his problems (yesterday's *Wall Street Journal*); and a gamer dude wearing a Pac-Man T-shirt whose Bright exploded with the sounds of an eternal arcade (handful of quarters). Unfortunately, not every Brightkey was as easy to identify. A boy wearing a base-ball cap had no interest in mitt or ball. In the teacher's room, a stern-looking old man wearing gardening gloves turned his nose at the trowel Cordelia laid at his feet.

Still, with ten minutes remaining until the end of the race, Cordelia could practically taste victory. She had freed two more ghosts than Agnes, who insisted on immediately cataloging each emancipated spirit in her database before she forgot the "relevant details," and remained only a single ghost behind Benji.

I can do this, Cordelia thought.

She paused to consider her next step. There were a couple of spirits nearby—a redheaded boy holding a wicker basket and a woman wearing a black bridal veil—but Cordelia wasn't very confident about the Brightkeys she had brought for them. What if she had guessed wrong? Trying to help them might be a total waste of time. On the other hand, she was fairly certain about the Brightkeys that would free the two ghosts haunting the attic—but she'd have to cross the entire school to get there, wasting precious minutes.

Take a chance? she wondered. Or go for the sure thing?

Cordelia headed toward the attic.

2

Halloween in July

Cordelia burst into the third-floor storage closet and pulled a hidden lever. A panel in the wainscoting clicked open, providing entrance to a dark, narrow passage that inclined toward the upper reaches of the school. Instead of rusting pipes and moldy insulation, as one might find in the innards of normal buildings, the bays framed elaborate wooden designs that resembled spiderwebs. Above Cordelia's head, copper wire linked a series of hollow black pyramids that stood like power stanchions. These pyramids could also be found in a similar passageway that started in the boiler room and coiled around the chimney like a snake.

Their purpose remained one of the many mysteries

of Shadow School.

But not for long, Cordelia thought. Now that we've found Elijah Shadow's office, it's only a matter of time before we unlock all of his secrets.

With the help of her trusty flashlight, Cordelia navigated the narrow passageway to a trapdoor that led into the attic. Beneath the slanted ceiling, rows of architectural models sat on wooden pedestals like an exhibit of dollhouses. The models ranged from lavish mansions to humble cabins. Each of them was the tiny twin of a house that had once existed in the real world.

Not a normal house. A haunted house.

Elijah Shadow, the namesake of Cordelia's school, had been a brilliant architect and an expert on ghosts. Unlike other authorities on the paranormal, however, he didn't believe that ghosts remained among the living because they were angry or restless. Instead, Elijah had theorized that certain houses were more hauntable than others due to specific architectural characteristics. He used this idea—which he called *archimancy*—to build the ultimate haunted house. Elijah lived there for the rest of his life, studying its spectral inhabitants, and many years after his death, the house became Shadow School.

As Cordelia could attest from firsthand experience, it was just as haunted now as it had been when Elijah had called it home.

Cordelia climbed the ladder and closed the trap-door behind her. She was relieved to see that Benji hadn't beaten her to the two ghosts haunting the attic: a little girl wearing a witch mask and carrying a plastic pumpkin, and an old man sitting on a chest, tapping his foot soundlessly against the floor.

She checked her phone.

Five minutes left, she thought. More than enough time to free both of them.

Cordelia decided to start with the trick-or-treater. After a solid minute of digging through her stuffed backpack, she finally managed to excavate a handful of soft miniature chocolates.

"Hey there," she said, kneeling so that she was eye level with the girl. She gently placed the chocolates in front of her. "These are for you. They're a little melty. Sorry about that."

The girl didn't seem to mind. She leaned forward, cobalt blue eyes widening behind the holes of her mask, and reached toward the chocolates. The neon light from the glow stick wrapped around her wrist grew in intensity.

Just as the ghost was about to touch the candy, Benji popped his head through the trapdoor. "Wait!" he exclaimed, taking stock of the situation as he scrambled into the attic. He hadn't gotten a haircut all summer, and his long, wavy hair flopped over his eyes. "You don't want those pathetic little things! I have the real deal!"

Benji produced a full-sized Hershey bar from a side pocket of his schoolbag and placed it on the floor. The trick-or-treater peeked over her shoulder and considered this new offering.

"Seriously?" Cordelia asked. "You're going to try to steal my ghost?"

"Don't blame me," Benji replied with an innocent shrug. "It was your idea to turn this into a competition."

"That was the only way I could get you to come! Ever since summer started, it's like you've totally forgotten about the ghosts."

Benji nodded. "It's called a vacation, Cord. You should give it a try."

The trick-or-treater took a few steps in Benji's direction, already reaching for the Hershey bar. "Good choice!" Benji said with a triumphant grin. Usually Cordelia liked his smile, but this one only served to annoy her further. *How can he act like he's better at rescuing ghosts than me when I had to make up this stupid game to get him here in the first place?* She was angry, no doubt about that, but also hurt that she'd had to work so hard to convince him. Even if Benji didn't care about the ghosts, hadn't he wanted to see her?

Cordelia pulled out a handful of chocolates, determined not to let him win. "One measly chocolate bar?" she asked the ghost. "Is that all he's got? I have four different flavors over here!"

The little girl turned to face Cordelia again and cocked her head to one side.

"Are those itsy-bitsy chocolates melted?" Benji asked. Cordelia was gratified to see that the grin had vanished from his face. "I kept mine in a freezer all night. Right now it's perfect."

"I have more!" Cordelia exclaimed, digging out new pieces of candy from the bottom of her bag. "Mr. Goodbar! Tootsie Roll!"

"Nobody likes Tootsie Rolls," Benji said. "Not even ghosts." He unwrapped a corner of the Hershey bar. "Here, I'll get this started for you."

The trick-or-treater turned from Benji to Cordelia, then back to Benji again. The plastic pumpkin shook in her trembling hand. *She's getting frustrated,* Cordelia thought. It wasn't the first time she had seen something like this happen. Sometimes ghosts got upset when she offered them too many incorrect Brightkeys.

That had always been an accident, though, Cordelia thought as the ghost spun back and forth indecisively. This is completely different. We're teasing this poor girl.

"We have to stop," Cordelia said, her cheeks warm with shame. "This is mean."

Benji, looking guilty, nodded in agreement. "We're sorry," he told the ghost. "Take any chocolate you want."

"Or take them all," Cordelia added. "The important thing is that you go into your—"

The neon bracelet wrapped around the ghost's wrist exploded in a blinding flash of green. Cordelia shielded her eyes and turned away. When she looked back again, the trick-or-treater was almost upon her: floating, arms outstretched, the tips of her black boots barely touching the floor. Spirits couldn't make physical contact with anything other than their Brightkeys and normally passed through the living with no ill effect. That changed when they were upset. They still couldn't touch the living, but the passage of their fingers through skin and bone left behind a cold, numbing sensation. Cordelia had been "stung" in this way a handful of times. The feeling passed in a few hours, but that didn't mean the ghosts weren't dangerous. Until this point, she had only been stung on her arms and legs. She didn't want to think about what might happen if a ghost's fingers ever passed through her heart.

Worried about just that possibility, Cordelia covered her chest as she leaped away from the trick-or-treater. She wasn't quite fast enough. The dead girl's